MISADVENTURES

IN THE

CAGE

MISADVENTURES

IN THE

CAGE

BY
SARAH ROBINSON

WATERHOUSE PRESS

ISBN: 978-1-64263-210-1

To Larry—you're an absolute dick.

CHAPTER ONE

"Oh, my God... Josie? Josie Gray?" A young woman with short black hair and a vibrantly metallic dress sidled up to her at the bar in O'Hannigan's Bar & Grill. "Can I please get a picture with you?"

Josie shot back the glass of tequila and then sucked on the lime, hissing as it hit her stomach hard. She was already four shots in, and each one was helping her forget the giant rejection letter she was carrying around in her purse.

We regret to inform you that the position of
sous chef is no longer available blah blah blah.

She got the point. She was never going to be a chef. Every job application she'd sent in over the last year had been turned down.

Not that she was allowed to do what she wanted.

"Sure," she replied, finally turning to the woman and putting on her best fake smile.

The woman held up her iPhone, turning the camera around to face them, and put on her best duck face as she posed next to Josie.

Josie just smiled and then turned back to the bar as soon as the photo was taken.

"Another one," she indicated to the bartender, but when she lifted her hand to motion, she knocked over her glass.

Thankfully, it didn't shatter, but it made a loud-ass noise as it clattered against the bar.

The bartender shook his head, casting her a pitying look. God, she hated that. "Miss Gray, I think you've had enough. Why don't I call you a cab?"

"No," she sighed loudly. Admittedly, she was getting tired and had probably had enough. Plus, she couldn't really afford *TMZ* writing an article about how the reality television star was wasted and falling all over herself at a local bar. Hell, it was the entire reason she'd come to this place off the strip to begin with—anonymity. So much for that. "I'll order a Lyft. Thank you, though."

She paid her check and then pulled out her phone to order a ride through a rideshare app. Honestly, she wasn't normally like this. She didn't regularly get drunk by herself at a bar off the Las Vegas strip in a seedy part of town.

Hell, this entire town was a seedy part of town, depending on how one looked at it.

She'd spent her entire life living in Las Vegas, though, so it was home to her. She was comfortable with its antics and qualms. Something about it . . . she could handle. At least, that was what she told herself.

Pulling her sweater up around her shoulders, she grabbed her purse and decided to wait for her Lyft out front. She could really use the still night air to sober her up before getting in a lurching car ride. God forbid she puke in the back of someone else's car.

She debated canceling the Lyft and just calling her driver, but then he would tell her brother where she'd been and she'd never hear the end of it. No, she needed the time off the clock and away from the freaking cameras.

"Hey, Miss," a voice called out to her as she stood on the front steps, trying to take some deep breaths. "You left this on the bar."

She turned to see an older gentleman, maybe twenty years her senior, approaching her. He was holding a tube of lipstick. She didn't recognize it, and it certainly wasn't hers. She never wore lipstick.

She shook her head. "That's not mine."

"Are you sure?" He frowned and then glanced back up at her. "I bet it would look real pretty on your chocolate skin."

Do I look like a damn candy bar to you?

Josie pulled her sweater tighter around her, hoping the Lyft would show up. "It's not mine," she repeated.

"Why don't you try it on?" he insisted. "Let's just test it out."

"No." She moved away from him, but he approached her faster.

"Just try it on, sweet thing." He grabbed her wrist and twisted it, yanking her backward. "I just want to see how it looks on ya."

"Let go of me!" she yelled, struggling to free her arm from his grasp.

"Don't be such an uppity little bitch," the man said, squeezing her wrist tighter and tighter until she cried out in pain. "I've seen you on TV before."

"Hey!" A fist came out of nowhere and landed squarely against the man's jaw.

He staggered back and released Josie's wrist, causing her to fall to the ground. He clutched his face. "What the hell?"

"The lady said let go," the owner of the fist—a tall, buff young man who looked like a brick wall stuffed in a suit—

instructed her attacker. "I suggest you listen to women when they talk. I'd also suggest you leave. Now."

The older man scurried away like a dog with his tail between his legs.

Josie wasn't sorry to see him go.

The newcomer turned back to her, concern etched on his features, his brow furrowed. "Are you okay?"

"I . . . I think so?" She got back up to her feet and examined her wrist, wincing at the pain.

He noticed her expression. "We need to get you to a hospital."

"No way. I'm not spending all night in a hospital room when I know it's not broken. It probably just needs some ice."

Plus, she couldn't afford the fallout from the media over yet another family scandal. It was bad enough that her entire family was on a reality television show, thanks to her brother's career that chronicled her every move, but knowing that any little thing she did could be used as fodder for an episode was a nightmare waiting to happen.

"See, I can still move it." She gingerly moved her wrist.

A small smirk played across his lips, and she couldn't help but notice a slight Irish lilt in his voice. "Useful."

"Th-Thank you for your help," she stammered, trying to find something to say to this incredibly gorgeous man who'd just ridden in like Prince Charming and saved her life. "I'll just go find my Lyft now."

"What's your name?" he asked, seeming to ignore everything she'd just said.

"Josie." It was a nice change of pace to run into someone who didn't know who she was. Although that wasn't very unusual with men because they weren't really the target demographic for her family's show.

He nodded. "I'm Callan."

"Nice to meet you, Callan." She started to walk away.

"Need a ride home?" he asked, motioning to a sleek black SUV parked against the curb. Of course, it had to be a freaking Range Rover.

Who the hell was this guy? It certainly wasn't unusual in Las Vegas to run into celebrities, but she didn't recognize him...although something about his face...he did look familiar.

She glanced down at her phone and checked her Lyft app. Her driver was still thirteen minutes away. *What the hell?* She canceled the ride.

"Sure. Why not?"

A ride with a life-saving potential celebrity sounded safer anyway than with a total stranger vetted only by an app. At least, that was the story she was going with to convince herself to get into the car with this drop-dead handsome man. And when she said drop-dead handsome, she meant it. The dude was gawk-worthy. Chiseled muscles on every inch of his body that she could see. Long, wavy brown hair tied back in a ponytail and blue eyes that made her knees feel like they were made of Jell-O.

"Is this your car?" she asked, motioning to the Range Rover.

He nodded and opened the passenger door for her. "Hop in."

"Hold on. One second." She walked around to the front of the car and took a picture of the car and license plate and sent it off in a quick text to her best friend, Emily.

"Did you just take a picture of my license plate?" he asked, one brow raised as he watched her.

"And texted it to my friend," she confirmed, waltzing past him and climbing into the passenger seat of the car.

He chuckled, leaning against the doorframe. "Can I ask why?"

"In case you murder me." She turned to face him, giving him a deadpan expression like it was the most obvious thing ever.

Her mother had taught her that trick years ago, though growing up in Las Vegas had been an education in and of itself. Men were a lot less likely to act nefariously when they knew they were being held accountable by an anonymous third party.

A grin spread wide across his face, and it only made his beautiful features all the more glorious. "Smart lady." He closed her car door, and she watched with interest as he walked around the car and then climbed into the driver's seat. The way he moved... Jesus, it was a sin. He stalked around the car like he was searching for prey, and it made her shiver—in the best way.

"Where to, Ms. Precaution?" he asked.

Maybe it was the tequila talking, or maybe it was the fact that he was daring her to throw caution to the wind, or maybe she was just fed up with the monotony of her life and wanted to throw a wrench into things. She wasn't sure what made the next words come out of her mouth. All she knew was that she'd said them and she didn't want to take them back...

"Take me to your place."

CHAPTER TWO

If there was one thing Callan hadn't expected tonight, it was to meet her. Tight black curls that fell loose around her face and bobbed as she talked, bright-green eyes that seemed to gaze right through him, creamy brown skin that he wanted to run his hands across... She was every bit as intoxicating as he'd suspected when he'd first seen her across the bar pounding back tequila shots.

He'd considered approaching her, but she'd looked deep in thought and not in the mood for company. By the time he'd decided to do it anyway, she was already leaving, but he'd seen an older man follow her out. He wasn't sure it was any reason for alarm, but he'd decided to check anyway just to be sure.

Thank God he had.

Now fifteen minutes later, she was asking him to take her to his house for the night.

"Don't tempt me like that, Josie," he replied, eyeing her sideways. "You're a beautiful girl, and that's a hard thing to turn down."

"So don't turn it down," she replied, like it was the most obvious answer. He already was loving her wit and attitude—the spunk in the way she spoke and viewed the world was mesmerizing.

"How do I know you're not drunk?" he asked, because hell if he was going to take advantage of a drunk woman.

She touched her fingers to her nose a few times and then

started counting backward from one hundred by sevens. He wasn't even sure if she was accurate, but she sounded right. Hell, she sounded sober enough.

"I'm telling you—the lipstick freak sobered me right the hell up," she assured him. "Now, let's go."

Callan smirked, enjoying the change of pace of being told what to do for once. Normally, he was the boss. He made the rules and laid down the law, but here was this tiny woman barking out orders, and he loved every second of it. And he was pretty sure he was going to love every second of tonight, too.

"You're a hard woman to say no to," he said, putting the car into gear and pulling out onto the main road. "And I don't think I want to."

She flashed her pearly whites at him in a wide grin. He returned her smile, already wanting to do more than that.

She reached over and began fiddling with the radio dials on his car. Finally, she stopped when she got to a station that was playing Cardi B. She leaned back against the passenger seat and began singing along, not getting a single lyric wrong. Her voice was fantastic, and he glanced sideways more than once to watch her bop along as they drove.

"Wait!" she suddenly screamed out. "Go back!"

"What?" Callan glanced in his rearview mirror, checking to make sure he hadn't hit anything.

"Did you see that?" Josie's head was halfway out the window, looking at something behind them.

"See what?" He was thoroughly confused.

"There's a woman lying on the ground over there." Josie pointed to a figure behind them lying across the sidewalk.

He could see it now that he'd slowed down.

There were no other cars on the road, so he slowed to a

stop and put the car in reverse. Pulling up next to the woman, he turned to Josie. "Stay here."

He had no idea if the situation was safe or not, and he wasn't about to risk her life on top of everything.

She nodded in agreement, green eyes wide.

Callan hopped out of the car and walked around to the figure. "Miss? Ma'am?"

The woman made no movement. *Shit.* He wasn't sure he could handle seeing a dead body. That certainly wasn't on his bucket list, and hell, his public relations manager would absolutely hate the nightmare this would cause for his career.

After gently tapping her shoulder, he moved his hands to her neck to feel for a pulse. "Miss, are you okay?"

Except there was no pulse.

Because it was a doll. One of the most realistic sex dolls he'd ever seen in his life. These things cost thousands of dollars, and this one was clearly well used and very . . . enjoyed.

"What the fuck?" Callan let out a loud laugh and then motioned for Josie to come join him. "Josie, it's a doll."

"What?" She scurried out of the car and over to him as he was flipping it over. It weighed over a hundred pounds—to be as realistic as possible—so she made a loud *thunk* when he flipped her onto her back.

"It's one of those human-like sex dolls." Callan had to admit, it was very realistic-looking and entirely creepy. He felt like he needed gloves to handle it because God knew where this doll had been or what had been done to it.

"Well . . . that's just sad," Josie said. "Leaving her like that, destitute and naked on the street. And, dang, what did they do to her lady parts? Poor girl has been through a lot."

"People are animals," he agreed, standing up and walking

back around to the driver's side of the car.

"Wait, we can't just leave her here," Josie said, calling him back. "She's so . . . real-looking. It's almost scary. We can't just abandon her on the side of the road like they did."

"What do you want to do with her? Toss her in the trash?" Callan grimaced because that didn't seem like the most humane option either. "Seems just as fucked up, to be honest."

"We have to give her a funeral and proper burial." Josie shrugged her shoulders, like it was the most normal thing in the world. "Sienna deserves that much."

"You want to bury her?" Callan tried not to laugh. "And she has a name now?"

Josie nodded. "Sienna the Sex Doll, yes. I want to bury her."

Callan tossed up his hands. "Sure. Why not? Let's bury a sex doll at midnight in Las Vegas."

She clapped her hands together. "Thank you! Come on, help me get her in the back of the car."

He glanced around again, hoping no one was watching. This was a photo-optics nightmare.

Opening the rear gate of his Range Rover, he reached in and grabbed a blanket he had stored back there. "Here. We can wrap her in this. I don't really want to be touching her anyhow."

"Shhh," Josie said, putting her finger to her lips. "Sienna might hear you."

Cool. So he was taking home a crazy chick. That was a fantastic twist to the evening.

Even more cause for alarm was the fact that his dick twitched at almost every word out of this crazy woman's mouth. There was something about her spirit that was having an effect on him he rarely experienced with other women.

Josie laughed. "I'm just kidding. Definitely don't touch her directly. That's herpes waiting to happen."

"I gathered as much," he assured her, tossing the blanket over the doll and wrapping it up. He lifted the faux body and placed her in the cargo space.

Josie watched him, helping tuck in the blanket as he stuffed the doll inside. "Well, if you ever needed to know if you could fit a body back here, the answer is yes."

"I'll be sure to tell the guy who sold me this car that he should start using that as a sales tactic," Callan said with a laugh as they both closed the back and walked around the car.

After hopping in, he pulled on his seat belt. "I can't believe I just stuffed a sex doll into my trunk."

"You're doing the right thing," Josie said solemnly, buckling herself in as he pulled away from the curb. "Sienna deserves a proper burial."

After a quick stop at a local hardware store—one that was closed but happened to have a rack of shovels on a stand outside that they could "borrow"—they headed out to the desert. As soon as they hit the city limits, Callan pointed around at the vast amount of empty space.

"Pick a spot, I guess?"

She motioned toward a lone bush in the middle of nowhere. "By that bush."

He pulled the car off the main highway and into the desert, rolling up by the bush. Gravel at the side of the road crunched under his feet as he reached into the back seat for the shovel.

He pointed next to the bush, which was illuminated only by the SUV's headlights. "Here?"

Josie nodded. "Do you want help?"

"Digging a human-sized hole when your wrist is all fucked

up?" He shook his head. "Nah, I got it."

Suddenly, Josie looked a little nervous and pulled out her phone. She was holding it like a lifeline.

Callan eyed her for a second. "Did you just put two and two together that you're in the middle of the desert with a virtual stranger, and he's digging a hole for a body?"

A small grin crossed Josie's lips. "The thought may have crossed my mind."

CHAPTER THREE

"This was *your* idea," Callan reminded Josie, laughing at the absurdity of the moment. They were standing in the desert burying a sex doll they'd found on the side of the street at midnight. They were virtual strangers themselves, and yet, here they were, bonding over the weirdest Vegas experience he was sure anyone had ever had.

Okay, so that probably wasn't true. But this was still weird as shit.

"Fair," she agreed, wrapping her arms around herself. "But let's hurry. It's cold out here."

Callan quickly dug a shallow hole big enough to squeeze Sienna's plastic body into. They tucked the blanket down into the earth together, and then he shoveled dirt back on top, covering her up. The entire process took about ninety minutes, because even working fast, digging in the hard sand was no easy effort.

"Great. Now we can go home?" he asked, finishing patting the dirt on top of the hole.

Josie shook her head. "We need to say a few words. Have a proper funeral."

"Good Lord, what the hell do you say at a sex doll's funeral?"

She cleared her throat and turned on the flashlight on her iPhone, pointing it at the burial site. "Sienna was well-loved, and her company was greatly enjoyed by all who met her."

Callan bit his lip to keep from laughing, and he could see a similar amusement on Josie's face as well. "Sienna's absence will forever leave a hole that no one can fill."

"Sienna, you really were a one-of-a-kind friend," Josie continued. "And someone, somewhere, will greatly miss you."

"Rest in peace," Callan finished. Then he made the sign of the cross over his forehead and chest. "Okay, I think it's safe to say she received a respectable funeral."

Josie nodded and then took his hand and gave it a squeeze. She let out a little laugh and shook her head. "We did a good thing."

His dick leaped in response at her touch. *Calm down, boy.* Apparently crazy was a turn-on for him because the battier this chick acted, the more he was attracted to her.

"Only in Vegas," he replied. "Come on. Let's get you back home."

He figured after the insanity of the night, there was no way she still wanted to come back to his place. Although he had to admit, now he wanted her even more than before.

She shook her head, climbing into the car next to him. "I just helped bury a body in the desert. I really don't think I should be alone tonight," she teased, poking his leg. "Let's go back to your place."

"Yeah?"

She grinned at him—big green eyes and a wicked smile that he knew was going to get him in trouble. "Yeah."

He pulled the car back onto the main highway and listened along as Josie blasted music again and sang along. After about thirty minutes, they were back in the middle of Las Vegas and headed toward their destination.

Josie reached over and turned down the music, looking

around. "Are we going to the strip?"

That was the other aspect he hadn't mentioned to her just yet. "Well, you said you wanted to go to my home. The MGM Grand is home for the next month. I don't live in Las Vegas. I'm actually from Los Angeles."

She nodded, taking on a contemplative expression. He wondered what she was thinking and debated asking her, but he liked the mystery of it all.

"What were you doing at a local bar?" she asked, tucking her feet up underneath her on the car seat and leaning her head back to look at him. "It's not often we get tourists down there."

Callan shrugged, pulling the car into the valet lane at the MGM. "I like to get away from the craziness of the strip every once in a while. Plus, when I'm visiting places, I love to explore the local watering holes and sites. Get a feel for the area and the people. Occasionally bury a sex doll in the desert. That sort of thing."

She seemed to like that answer, because she got a dreamy look on her face, her eyes softening and a small smile forming on her lips. The car came to a stop, and she unbuckled her seat belt, hopping out her side of the car before he had the chance to walk around and open the door for her.

"Welcome back, Mr. Callan, sir." The valet took his keys and hopped into the driver's seat.

He nodded. "Thank you."

After walking around the car, he rejoined Josie on the curb in front of the hotel. She stepped next to him and slid her hand into his, wrapping her fingers around his. He glanced down at their hands and tried to hold back a smile, but it was pointless. There was something so comfortable, so sweet about the gesture.

He was warming to her, and he barely even knew her.

They made their way through the casino and toward the hotel elevators. He noticed she kept her head down and pointed away from the cameras, but he didn't ask her why. People liked their privacy—especially in a place like Vegas.

"Want to play the slots?" he asked, nodding toward some of the machines.

She grinned. "I'm a good-luck charm, you know that?"

Something about the way she said it, he believed her wholeheartedly. "Are you?"

"Yeah, but I don't want to play tonight. Not those games, anyway." She smirked and then let her gaze travel down the length of his body as they waited for the elevator.

He nearly blushed at the way she was looking him over, but fuck, it felt powerful. Knowing she wanted him like that . . . so openly, so hungrily. He pressed the elevator button again so it would hurry the hell up.

Finally, the doors opened, and they stepped inside. He pressed the button for his floor, and her brows shot up.

"Penthouse?" she asked, one hand on her hip.

He shrugged his shoulders but otherwise didn't respond. There was no way he was going to tell her who he was and mess up the vibe going on between them. What if she was a fan? Or was only interested in him for his fame and fortune? He couldn't take the risk. Plus, he liked the anonymity of the evening so far.

He wasn't really one for one-night stands. He'd only had a handful of them before in his life. It wasn't that he hadn't enjoyed them—hell, he definitely had. It was just that he was focused on his work and wasn't one to let women or dalliances get in the way of that.

So why was he saying yes tonight?

Josie wasn't a woman to say no to.

Instead, he decided to break the silence with what he did best. Moving closer to her, he took her face in his hands and kissed her. Her eyes fluttered to a close, and she let out the softest sigh he'd ever heard. It was sweet and sensual, and it made his entire body harden and melt all at the same time.

The elevator doors opened, and they broke apart as they entered a short hallway before he let them into his penthouse suite. She glanced around briefly but didn't seem too shocked by the interior or glamour of the space.

He was a little disappointed because he had expected some *oohs* and *aahs* about how amazing his suite was, but she seemed right at home, like she'd been here a thousand times before.

After shrugging off her coat, she laid it over the back of a velvet couch. "Bedroom is through here, right?" She pointed to a hallway off the side.

He nodded, wondering for the hundredth time what her story was. He had to admit, he was a little worried that she seemed so at home in the MGM's penthouse suite. He'd never slept with a hooker before, and he wasn't about to change that streak tonight.

"Been here before?" he asked.

Josie nodded. "Well, not this exact penthouse, but similar ones. My brother travels a lot for work, and we get to stay in pretty nice places on the strip for his job."

Relief flooded him at the explanation. "Ah, so what does your brother do? Hell, what do you do? I don't know anything about you."

She waved her hands in front of her. "Let's set some ground rules."

"I'm game." He walked over to the bar cart and poured them both a glass of whiskey neat. "What is the first rule?"

She lifted one finger in the air. "No last names."

"So tonight is just . . . tonight?" he confirmed.

Josie shrugged. "Maybe. Maybe we can exchange numbers later . . . I haven't decided yet."

A smirk played on Callan's lips. There she went again . . . making all the rules. He was just a puppet in her game. Little did she know, he was about to take control the moment they hit that mattress.

A second finger lifted. "Rule number two: Strawberry."

He raised one brow. "What?"

"That's my safe word," she clarified. "Strawberry."

His cock twitched in his jeans. Holy hell, the little minx was clearly ready for almost anything he was more than willing to provide. The surprises kept coming.

As calmly as he could, he cleared his throat and nodded his head. "Strawberry. Got it."

"Third rule," she continued, lifting one more finger. "You can't fall in love with me."

The whiskey he was swallowing went down the wrong way, and he fell into a fit of coughing and sputtering.

"You okay?" she asked.

He coughed again, nodding as he pounded a fist to his chest. After clearing his throat, he finally managed to choke out a few raspy words. "Yeah, I'm okay. I think we're safe on that last rule, though."

He'd never been in love, and he had no plans on falling in love tonight. It was absolutely hilarious, though, that she felt the need to list it in her rules. This woman was becoming more and more intriguing by the minute.

It was Josie's turn to smirk now. "Laugh all you want, but those are my rules."

Callan took a seat in one of the high-back chairs by the long wall of windows overlooking the lights of the strip. Finishing off the last of his whiskey, he placed his glass down and then folded his arms over his chest.

"Are you done listing off your rules?" he asked simply.

A hint of nervousness crossed her expression, but she masked it quickly. He saw it, though, and what she didn't realize was that this was a game of cat and mouse...and she was the mouse.

"Yes," she replied.

"Good. Then I have a few rules for you."

She turned her body to squarely face his but didn't sit down. She liked being taller than him, he could sense. She liked that power. He knew that about her already.

He was going to bring her to her knees.

"Rule number one," he began. "You may address me only as 'sir' tonight."

Her lips pursed, and he couldn't tell if she agreed or not, but she stayed quiet.

"Rule number two," he continued. "You come when I tell you and *only* when I tell you."

Her tongue slid out of her mouth and ran across her lower lip.

"And lastly, rule number three," he finished. "From now until tomorrow morning, you are mine to do with as I please. Whatever I please."

"Callan..." Her voice was hoarse and throaty.

"If you don't agree to my rules, I'll have a driver take you home now. No problem, no consequences," he assured her.

"But tell me now."

She paused, her eyes darting toward the door they'd entered through and then back to him. Her chin tilted up slightly, and he knew her answer.

"I agree to your terms," she replied.

Thank fucking God.

CHAPTER FOUR

Josie watched as Callan picked up a tablet on the table beside his chair and pressed a few buttons. Soft music came on, the room lights dimmed, and candles flickered all around them.

A gentle glow cast against his pale Irish skin, and she loved the way he looked in the candlelight. His hair was darker now that he had pulled it out of its ponytail, allowing it to hang freely around his face. It looked so soft. She wanted to run her fingers through it.

"Give me a minute to clean up," he told her, heading for the bathroom.

To be fair, he had been digging in the dirt for ninety minutes.

She stayed in the center of the room, waiting for him. Her body felt like it was on fire and only he could quench her blaze.

He returned moments later, freshly washed and wearing nothing but a pair of sweatpants.

My God, those abs.

His body was incredible, and she nearly fell apart just staring at him. He took a seat in the chair across from her, still keeping distance between them.

"Take off your clothes," he instructed. His tone was kind but commanding. There was no option in his voice. It was do it now or leave, and she wanted nothing more than to strip bare every inch of clothing from her body in front of his gaze. She wanted him to see her naked. She wanted him to see every inch of her.

Slowly, she reached for the hem of her shirt, lifted it above her head, and dropped it onto the floor. Then she unfastened the button to her jeans and unzipped them, sliding them down her legs and shimmying out of them before kicking them to the side.

She kept her eyes on his, watching him as he watched her.

Stepping out of her heels, she reached behind her body for her bra strap. Finding the hook, she unfastened it and let the lacy fabric fall from her breasts to the floor. She heard the sharp intake of his breath at the exposure of herself to him. Her stomach fluttered at his audible response, and her pulse quickened. But she kept going.

After sliding her panties down her legs next, she stepped out of them and revealed herself entirely nude to him. When she turned her gaze back to Callan, it was hard not to notice the bulge in his pants or the heated fire in his eyes.

"You're incredibly beautiful," he murmured barely loud enough for her to hear, but she heard him anyway. "Come here."

She walked over slowly and came to a stop in front of him. He placed his hands on her hips and ran them down the length of her thighs and back up again. Leaning forward and closer to her, he slid his tongue in a circle around her right nipple and then her left. She arched her back to be closer to him, her eyes closing at the sensation.

"Oh, God . . ." she moaned.

He bit down slightly, and she squeaked, a sharp pain radiating out across her chest. Mixed with the pleasure of feeling his hands on her, it was an intoxicating combination. When his fingers found their way between her legs, she stiffened . . . but then parted and welcomed him.

Every stroke of his finger against her, his hands holding her, made her want to collapse in his arms. She wanted more. She wanted him to push her over the edge she'd been teetering on ever since she first saw him.

"You're soaking wet." He chuckled lightly as he leaned back in his chair and looked up at her. "I don't think I'll ever get enough of you, Josie."

She panted, staring down at his beautiful big eyes, chewing on her bottom lip. Those eyes—she could get lost in them. There was a fire behind the darkness, and she wanted to bathe in everything he was offering her. She had a sneaking suspicion that not many people saw this side of him—the vulnerability he was letting her into.

"Go sit on that couch across from me," he instructed, removing his hands.

She balked. "What?"

"The correct answer is 'yes, sir.'"

Josie swallowed and took a deep breath. Her entire body was tingling with a combination of fear and excitement, but the last thing she wanted to do was hold back.

"Yes, sir." She walked to the couch in front of him and sat down, acutely aware of his stare.

"Spread your legs and put your feet up on either side of you on the couch," he instructed, motioning to her legs.

She did as she was told, blatantly exposing herself to him. She was almost embarrassed, but something about the way his eyes feasted on her gave her a sense of . . . power. She felt adored, and she liked that.

"Touch yourself. I want to watch you pleasure yourself," he told her, pushing his sweatpants down. "Watch me do the same."

When his cock sprang free, her eyes nearly bulged out of her head. It was freaking massive. Hell, there was no way she was going to sit all the way over here and not enjoy that cock all night.

"But..."

He lifted one brow, and that was all he needed to do to remind her of who made the rules here. He had been very clear. It was his rules for the rest of the night. She was his to do with as he pleased until tomorrow morning, and if she didn't like it ... well, she didn't have to be here.

And she *really* wanted to be here.

Sliding a hand between her legs, she found her wet slit and ran her fingers up and down it. The sensation almost caused her to buck off the couch because of how sensitive she'd become just from the way he was staring at her.

He gripped his cock and began rubbing his hand up and down. A low growl emanated from his throat when he watched her dip a finger inside herself and then two. They went on like that for a while, rubbing and thrusting and pushing themselves closer and closer to the edge with their eyes glued to one another.

Josie's fingers found her clit, and she began rubbing quick, hard circles over the sensitive bundle of nerves. "I'm close," she said with a gasp as she felt her orgasm rumbling beneath the surface.

"Stop."

"What?" She stopped rubbing and looked at him, her body protesting the abrupt halt. She was full of tension, and her release was just out of grasp.

"Come here." He lifted one finger and curled it, calling her toward him. "You don't come without me."

She could get behind that. Scurrying off the couch, she quickly made her way over to him, but as soon as she reached him, he turned her around and then placed a hand on her back. He pushed her down until she was bending over.

"Grab your ankles," he told her. "Spread your feet and come fucking hard."

He was still seated in the chair in front of her, and now she was spread wide in front of him like a goddamn feast. And he ate his fill. His tongue plunged between her folds and lapped at her core while his fingers twirled circles around her clit. Within seconds, she was bursting at the seams as her orgasm ripped through her, and she nearly fell to the rug beneath her feet.

He held her steady as he continued to lick, suck, nibble, and tongue fuck her orgasm out of her until she finally fell limp into his lap. He didn't miss a beat. Without pause, he'd already slid a condom onto his cock and sat her directly onto himself.

Gripping her waist with both hands, he lifted her off him and back on over and over, and he used his hips to pump in and out of her. She tilted her head sideways to find his mouth, their lips molding together as he kissed her.

Hard and fast, he thrust until she could feel the warm surge of his climax inside her and he groaned at his release. He stilled as he caught his breath, and she leaned back against his chest to catch her own.

"Fuck," he said with a slow groan. "That was amazing."

"And just think . . ." she teased. "We haven't even made it to the bedroom yet."

CHAPTER FIVE

"I've never seen anyone cook naked before," Callan commented, leaning against the island counter in the hotel suite's kitchen as Josie stood in front of the range in nothing but an apron.

"I'm technically wearing an apron," she pointed out, jostling the string around her waist. "So, I'm not naked. Safety first, you know."

He chuckled, picking up the glass of whiskey in front of him and sipping on it. "What are you making anyway?"

As soon as they'd recovered from their third bout of having sex, she'd declared she was famished and needed sustenance. Literally. That was how she'd said it. He'd offered her room service—hello, this was the MGM—but she'd insisted on cooking something herself. Luckily, he had a fully stocked fridge, so that wasn't a concern.

"Breakfast," she replied.

He glanced down at his Rolex. It was almost three in the morning. "Well, I guess it *is* almost morning."

Josie turned her head to look back at him, a dashing smile on her face. "Breakfast for late-night dinner is one of the best luxuries in life."

"The hotel does serve food all day long to the penthouse, you know," he reminded her as he walked up behind her and circled his arms around her waist. She leaned her head to the side as he kissed her neck. "We could have had this ordered in . . . to bed."

She swatted him away. "There's still plenty of time for that. I just love to cook. I was going to be a chef, you know."

He leaned back against the counter. "Were you?"

She nodded. "I was. Until my brother's career kind of took center stage in my family."

"What's your brother's career have to do with you?" he asked as she plated an omelet and placed it in front of him. It had to be the fluffiest, most delectable stack of eggs and cheese he'd ever smelled.

"What happened to our rules?" She lifted one brow as she looked up at him. "No details, remember."

"Humor me," he responded.

Indecision crossed her face, but she finally shrugged her shoulders. "I work for my brother."

She stabbed a fork into his omelet and took a bite for herself.

He surveyed her face as she spoke and noticed a flicker of something—resentment, annoyance? He wasn't sure, but it seemed negative. He wanted to dig a little deeper.

"Is that your dream job?"

She snorted, rolling her eyes so hard that they practically rolled into the back of her head. "Far from it. Like I said, I wanted to be a chef. I actually went to culinary school straight out of college. I have the skills to be one if I wanted. I just need to study under a chef for a while and get some experience in a kitchen—if any damn place would actually hire me. My real dream is to work on the strip one day or have a restaurant out in Los Angeles."

"Really?" That news perked up his ears. His hometown. "Los Angeles would be lucky to have you."

She handed him her fork, and he took a bite of the omelet.

The taste was every bit as good as how the eggs looked in their presentation. Better, even. The flavors teased and exploded against his tongue with every bite—a mixture of cheese and bacon and egg that worked perfectly together.

"Mmm." He closed his eyes. "Yeah, we'd be fucking thrilled to have you. You're talented, Josie. You should be doing what you love. You should be cooking."

"Maybe one day." She shrugged, sauntering back to the refrigerator, where she pulled out a carton of orange juice and poured a glass. She took a sip first and then placed it in front of him.

Callan offered her another bite of the large omelet because it was way too much for him to eat alone. She accepted, and he fed it to her. It was damn near sensual, and he realized he was getting turned on again just at the way her lips wrapped around the fork and pulled at the eggs.

"Fuck, that's hot," he said with a low growl coming up from his chest.

She grinned. "Do you want me to blow on it for you?"

There was no other way to answer that question except *hell fucking yes.*

With deliberate movements, he slowly pushed down the top of his sweatpants. He worked himself out of his boxer briefs and held his cock in his hands.

Her eyes widened as she watched him, and she visibly swallowed, her chest rising and falling faster and faster as her breath quickened.

"Get on your knees."

"Is that a command," she dared him, her eyes sparkling with desire and the hint of a smile on her lips. "*Sir?*"

"Get. On. Your. Knees." He would only repeat himself once.

Sauntering over to him, she placed her hands on his chest and slowly dropped to her knees, letting her hands slide down his chest as she did so. Her nails grazed his abs and stopped at the hem of his sweatpants, finding a resting spot on his hips.

"Mmm," she moaned as she leaned forward and let her tongue slide across the length of his hardened cock.

He hissed at the warm, wet sensation of her mouth, his hips bucking forward at the feeling. He moved deeper into her mouth, the warmth of her lips covering him as she took him deeper and deeper. Within seconds, he was sliding down her throat and then pulling back out, only to slide back down again.

The woman had no gag reflex. It was incredibly sexy, and he couldn't stop himself from taking full advantage of wanting every delicious lick of her tongue. She swirled around him like she was licking a lollipop, and he knew he was close.

"I'm close," he told her, warning her, but she just pulled him tighter against her.

When he came, she took everything he had to offer and then stood up like it was no big deal. He had to sit down at the kitchen island to collect himself, but she leaned against the counter and helped herself to the rest of the omelet like she was famished from a workout.

"You're amazing, you know that?" he said.

She chuckled. "Oh, I know. But wait until I make you my soufflé. You'll never be the same."

He lifted one brow. "Is that so?"

Josie finished her food and washed the plate, yawning and stretching her arms over her head.

"Ready for bed?" he asked.

Sheepishly, she glanced at him. "Honestly, a little bit. Maybe a short nap?"

Callan grinned, reaching a hand out toward her. "Come on, little one. Let's go to bed."

She took his hand and curled up into his side. He wrapped an arm around her, and they walked to the bedroom. He pulled the covers down on the mattress and watched as she crawled into the middle of the bed, taking the apron off and throwing it onto the floor.

Callan rid himself of his sweatpants, leaving him in only his boxer briefs, and crawled into the king-size bed beside her.

The big spoon to her little spoon, he wrapped his body around hers from behind. She sighed contentedly and backed up into him.

"Good night, Callan," she said with a soft whisper, kissing the back of his hand.

"Good night, Josie," he replied, kissing the side of her head through her curly mound of hair. "Thanks for tonight."

She giggled. "You're welcome?"

"I'm serious," he said. "There's no one else I'd rather bury a body with. I'm really glad we met."

"Aw." She turned around in his arms to face him, chest to chest, laughing lightly at his words. "I'm really glad we met, too. I feel really close to you already. We're basically bonded for life now over that damn doll."

He grinned. "Partners in crime."

She pushed a lock of hair out of his face and smoothed her finger across his cheek. "I feel like we were meant to meet."

"Maybe we were," he mused.

"Maybe we were," she confirmed.

CHAPTER SIX

When she woke up the next morning, Josie could feel the ache of the tequila pounding in her skull. She groaned, rubbing at her temples as she tried to focus on a way to make the pain go away.

"Not feeling so hot?" Callan asked her, yawning as he was just coming around to waking up. His arms were wrapped around her torso. "All that tequila yesterday would do it."

Josie made a moaning sound in response because that was about all she could manage at the moment. She backed up into his body farther, curling into his warmth.

"I'm taking that as a 'not feeling so hot,'" he replied, gently peeling himself from her and standing up from the bed. "Can I get you anything? Water? Aspirin?"

"Yes and yes." She put her head under a pillow and blocked out the sunlight streaming in through the window. "And anything else you can find to fix a hangover."

Memories of last night came swarming back to her. *Did we bury a sex doll together?* Oh, God. She needed to stop drinking.

Callan snorted, laughing. "How about some French toast and strawberries from room service?"

"Ding ding ding," she replied, sticking a hand up in the air. "I'll take two."

"Great, well, I'll place the order." He picked up the phone on the nightstand. "Stay as long as you'd like. I have a work obligation at eleven, so I have to leave in a few minutes."

"Where's my phone?" Josie scrambled out of bed so fast, she nearly rocketed from the sheets. "It's not eleven already, right?"

"It's ten o'clock," he informed her, checking the time on his iPhone. "We definitely slept in."

"Shit. Shit. Shit." She ran to the bathroom and turned the shower knobs quickly. "Mind if I take the fastest shower in the world?"

"Go for it," he told her. "So, is that a no on breakfast?"

"No time!" she shrieked, jumping under the stream of water and beginning to clean herself as fast as her hands could lather soap across her body. She had less than an hour to be clean, dry, and sitting with her brother at his press junket in front of hundreds of reporters. He was going to freaking kill her if she wasn't there. Hell, he was already probably freaking out that she wasn't at the house. She'd definitely missed the morning call time, having already supposed to be mic'ed-up and in front of the cameras this morning.

Shit. She was in deep shit.

Why did she even care? She paused for a moment, almost considering crawling right back into bed and fucking the hell out of the beautiful stranger she'd just met.

That would certainly be better than living her life. More like, living her brother's life. But she did what she had to do for the family. That was just part of being a Gray. It was the only life she had ever known.

She quickly finished up the rest of her shower and hopped out, drying herself off and looking for her clothes. She'd tossed them everywhere last night.

"Here," Callan said, walking up to her with a garment bag. "I had the hotel send this up while you were in the shower. I think it's your size."

She blinked twice, looking at him with surprise. "What?"

He unzipped the garment bag, and inside was a very professional-looking sleeveless white dress that cut off at the knees. "I figured you were late for a work event or something, and maybe this would come in handy. Seems like it would work for any type of event, really."

It was freaking perfect. Now she would actually look like she had tried for the press junket and not just rolled out of bed and done the walk of shame.

She balked at the grandness of the gesture. "You're just going to give me this?"

"I mean . . . you can bring it back," he said, a teasing smile on his lips. "I'd love an excuse to see you again."

Josie grinned, loving the not-so-subtle way he'd managed to sneak himself back into her life. "I think I would be willing to return the outfit tonight. I might need some help unzipping it, after all."

"I'm very good at taking off clothes," he teased with a wink.

She laughed, taking the dress from him and bringing it into the bathroom. She slipped on the dress and glanced at her reflection. It fit perfectly, like a glove. In fact, she looked downright amazing. She was definitely going to see him tonight, but she might not give this dress back—she looked too damn good in it.

Upon exiting the bathroom, she wrapped her arms around his neck and kissed him squarely on the lips. "Thank you. You're amazing."

He lifted her off the ground, growling lightly against her neck. Walking her over to the bed, he threatened to toss her onto it.

Josie squealed and smacked at his shoulders. "Put me down! I have to go!"

"Just one more romp in the sheets," he teased. "You're so fucking sexy in this dress."

She wiggled out of his arms, finally freeing herself. "You are impossible."

"Because I can't wait to see you again?" He kissed her on the cheek. "Some would call that romantic, my dear."

"Don't forget the rules," she reminded him, a flutter of nerves—or was it excitement?—in her belly. "No falling in love."

"I didn't make any promises about not falling in lust." He smacked her ass as she walked away, making an *mmm* noise. "That booty, though."

She laughed, putting an extra sway in her walk to purposely make her ass shake as she moved. "Goodbye, Callan."

"Goodbye, Josie," he called after her as she left the hotel room. "See you tonight. Same time, same place."

She waved at him and headed down the hallway. The moment she got on the elevator, she powered up her cell phone. Sure enough, it beeped for a solid minute with notifications coming in.

37 unread text messages.

10 missed calls.

3 voicemails.

Ah, her work was never done. Being her brother's personal assistant was exhausting sometimes, but it paid the bills. And it paid *well*. Like, really well. Almost as well as being one of the characters on *Gray's Angels*, the reality show that she and her family often starred in, even though her brother was the main character. Being his assistant and sister meant she had a main role in his life and, therefore, a main role on the show.

She was able to afford a really nice life in the city she loved because of what her brother did, and for that, she was really grateful. None of them would have found fame or success if it hadn't been for his career and bringing them to the limelight. She just had to remember that. She had to keep that in the foreground of her mind instead of thinking about all the what-ifs, the maybe-insteads, the I-could-have-beens.

Sure, she loved to cook, and she'd done damn well in culinary school, but that wasn't going to pay the bills anytime soon. Not here in Las Vegas, at least. Not to mention the fact that leaving the family business—which would essentially mean leaving her brother—would be seen as abandoning the family. Plus, she had a contract with the show.

Leaving just wasn't an option in the Gray family.

You do for family. It was the family motto, and if they had a crest, that was what it would say.

Josie picked up the phone and dialed her brother's number. "Hey, Xav."

Xavier Gray nearly burst through the phone, he was so loud. "Where the hell are you, Josie? It's nearly time for the press junket. You know I need you by my side for this. Plus, filming started hours ago. Aston is furious."

Aston was their producer and the man who'd helped launch her family into the public spotlight.

"I'm here! I'm at the hotel. I'll be there in less than five minutes." And that was the goddamn truth. The luck of the dice that Callan was staying at the same hotel that Xavier's press junket was at was astronomical. She couldn't believe it when he'd told her last night, and she had been thrilled at the coincidence.

"Thank fucking Christ," Xavier said through the phone. "Listen, I need a water and a breakfast sandwich. Can you hook your brother up?"

"Not a problem," she assured him, stepping off the elevator and heading toward a breakfast cart in the lobby. "Grabbing it now."

"You're the best, Jos." He hung up the phone without saying goodbye. His usual style.

Josie grabbed a few breakfast sandwiches—she knew the drill; everyone in the family was going to want one—and some waters from the breakfast cart and then headed to the conference room where the press junket was going to be held.

Her family was in a smaller conference room behind the main one, waiting to be introduced and led out onto the stage.

"Josie!" Xavier called out to her, waving her over to the waiting area where he was seated with their younger brother, Marcus, and their mother, Shondra. A crew of cameramen, sound men, and production assistants bustled around them.

Their father, Xavier Sr., wasn't in attendance today, which was fairly normal for him. He got anxious in large crowds, not being a people person. He rarely came to large events—or any, really—and the family had gotten accustomed to that.

Marcus immediately grabbed two breakfast sandwiches from her for himself. Typical.

"You could say thank you, you know," Josie reminded him, giving him every bit of attitude he deserved as she let the production assistant begin putting a microphone on her.

"Thank you," he said, or something like that. She could hardly tell because he was talking with a mouth full of egg and cheese biscuit.

Josie just rolled her eyes as she passed out the remaining biscuits to Xavier and her mother and waited for the sound guy to finish setting her up with a microphone for the cameras. A makeup artist rushed over to her and quickly began fixing her face as well, which she was grateful for because she didn't really want to be on camera looking like she'd just rolled out of some stranger's bed.

"Thanks, baby girl," Shondra said, squeezing her shoulder. "Is this a new dress? You look stunning, darling."

"It is," she confirmed. "Just wanted to do a little something special for the junket. I know what a big deal this is to Xavier."

Xavier nodded his approval. "Okay, let's go over what the topics are. Remind me?"

"You're more than prepared for this, but yeah, let's do a quick recap," Josie agreed. "They're going to ask you how you feel coming out of your last win in the fight against Yoel Romero. They're going to ask if you're prepped and ready for the fight against Walsh next week. They're going to ask you about your training regimen and what strategies you plan to use in the octagon against Walsh, especially being that Walsh hasn't lost a match yet."

"He's going to lose against me," Xavier said with a confident grin, pounding a fist against his chest. "Motherfucker is going to get his ass kicked all around that cage."

Her brother had quickly become one of the best UFC fighters in the league over the last five years, and he was on par to become the best. He was short and stocky and absolutely bulked to the max with muscles. He was like a brick wall in the octagon when an opponent came at him. It made him difficult to beat, and he had won fight after fight until he found himself making millions off a single event.

Hence, why he'd hired Josie to be his assistant. Hell, he had two other assistants on top of her, so it wasn't like he even needed her, but he relied on her for personal things. Plus, she was part of the show. She was his sister, after all.

It was a blessing, to be honest. The money he'd earned had brought their parents out of lower-middle class and put them into a beautiful home, where they never had to work again. It paid for her younger brother's college and had paid for her culinary school. She was so grateful to her brother for that and for the way he took care of all of their family.

The problem was, there was this invisible debt owed to him that she just could never seem to pay back. Except she was paying it back . . . with her life and service. Being a public figure came with a responsibility she just couldn't turn away from, as much as she wanted to sometimes.

"Gray . . . Ready?" a production assistant called into the back conference room, motioning for them to join the main conference room.

"Ready to put your game face on?" Josie asked. "Remember, this is your first time meeting Walsh. You've got to be intimidating. Strong."

"Show no fear." Xavier let out a growl and clenched his fists, looking angrier and angrier by the second. "I'm fucking pumped! Let's do this damn thing!"

He stormed into the next room with Josie a few steps behind. The back conference room gave access to one side of the platform where they'd be facing the reporters. They rounded the corner at the same time Walsh rounded the corner from the other side, looking just as angry, looking just like . . .

What the hell?

Josie's jaw dropped as she paused in her tracks and stared

at the man storming toward them from the other side of the stage.

Walsh was . . . Callan.

CHAPTER SEVEN

Callan faltered in his step, pausing for a moment as he marched onto the stage. *What the fuck is Josie doing here?* Panic immediately set in—had this all been a setup?

His opponent for next week's match, Xavier Gray, saw him hesitate slightly. A wicked grin split wide across his face like the smug bastard knew then and there that he had Callan beat.

Shit.

He couldn't afford the distraction. He couldn't afford that recognition in his opponent's eyes. One moment of weakness— even now, before they ever entered the cage—could signal the end of the fight if his enemy smelled it on him.

Shoving the image of her gorgeous fucking body in that white dress waltzing toward him to the back of his mind, Callan decided to pretend she didn't exist. She was a problem for another moment, but right now? No. He couldn't handle the thought process of wondering why she was here or how she looked so damn good even on so little sleep.

And damn, she looked amazing.

There was a moment before she noticed him that he just got to watch her walk next to Xavier Gray—her hips swinging from side to side—that absolutely made him lose his breath. His mind flashed back to everything they'd been through in the past twelve hours and how amazing she felt beneath him without any clothes between them.

Then she saw him.

Guilt. Her expression was unmistakable. She regretted their evening—she regretted him. She leaned closer toward Xavier and averted her eyes, as if trying to be unseen.

Had he just slept with his opponent's girl? And not just any opponent, but Xavier Gray? Main character of *Gray's Angels*? He'd never watched their reality show, but he had no doubt she was on it if she was part of his life.

That mistake could cost him his career.

He silently cursed himself for being so weak as to let a woman tempt him like she had last night. Hell, she hadn't really tempted him so much as he'd chased after her. Literally. He'd wanted her and he knew it. But to be so reckless and get entangled with a reality television star who was dating his opponent? So close to one of the biggest fights of his life?

He was undefeated for a reason. He let nothing get in between him and the cage. He'd been one of the highest-ranking fighters in the UFC for a year now, climbing his way to the top. He was a newcomer in all regards, especially considering that this was his first championship, but fighting was his life and his livelihood, and he was one hundred percent invested. He did nothing halfway. He was here to prove that he could defeat the greats, and so far, he had.

But Xavier Gray?

That was a beast even he wasn't sure he could handle. But he was damn sure going to try his hardest to prove that he deserved the title.

"Welcome Xavier Gray and Callan Walsh," a host said into the microphone at the podium in the center of the stage. The suited man pointed toward a microphone poised in the middle of the aisle in the room filled with reporters and news outlets. "Please line up at the microphone in the front row to ask your questions."

People swarmed to the microphone and began lining up quickly.

Xavier Gray was already taking his seat at the opposing table, Josie by his side.

Callan quickly moved to take his seat next, propping his elbows up on the tabletop and leaning in closer to the microphone pointed directly at him.

"First question is for Xavier Gray," a reporter asked from the aisle. "Are you worried about losing your title to the newcomer next week?"

Xavier grinned and looked dead center at Callan. "Not even a little."

"Same question to Callan Walsh," said the host, taking charge and directing the question around to him.

The crowd shifted their gaze to him, and all of a sudden, he felt the weight of his entire career. This moment. This fight. It was everything he'd been working toward. Anxiety started to creep up in his gut.

Where the hell is this coming from?

He never got nervous about public speaking, and he'd certainly never been shy in front of cameras. But seeing the woman he'd just slept with on the arm of his opponent? Fuck . . . it was messing with his head in a big way.

Swallowing hard, he reaffirmed his decision to ignore Josie entirely. She wasn't even here. She wasn't even a thought in his head. Hell, he'd been trained to tune out the distractions in his career—and he was going to do that now, starting with her.

"He's held on to his title long enough," Callan spoke

clearly and stoically into the microphone. "It's time someone takes it from him."

The crowd rustled with excitement, and Xavier visibly bristled at his response.

His opponent leaned in to his microphone.

"Wishful thinking on the rookie's part," Xavier said to the cameras, pandering to his audience, who were eating it up.

They went on like that for the next hour. Back and forth bickering—challenging each other more and more to bigger and loftier goals in the cage next week—while the reporters threw out questions to them, asking about their history, their records, and their upcoming match.

When it was finally time to come off stage, Callan had successfully ignored Josie for at least the last forty-five minutes and was completely pumped up with adrenaline from the verbal sparring match.

"Great job, Cal," Samson, his assistant, said, praising him after he walked down the stage steps and exited to the side. Cal was the name he normally went by and what the world knew him as. Callan was his full name, but only the people in his personal life knew that.

"That was perfectly on script," Samson continued. "The reporters ate it up. I'm watching the news outlets now, and viewers are responding favorably to the story of an up-and-comer taking the belt from Old Faithful in there. Seems he's not very well-liked."

"Probably because of his recent DUI," Callan confirmed with a nod. "Don't win a lot of favor that way after what happened to that poor woman and her child."

Xavier Gray had recently covered the tabloids when he'd driven drunk and hit a minivan with a mother and her child. They'd been severely injured, and he'd nearly gone to jail, but fame and money had wormed his way out of any real consequences.

Samson cringed but nodded his head in agreement. "As horrible as it is, the narrative works in our favor. He's disliked, and we're the good guys coming to take the crown from an evil king."

Callan grinned. "Not often I'm referred to as the good guy."

"Apparently," a voice said behind him.

He turned around and faced Josie. Her black hair was pushed back behind her ears, curls springing loose in every direction, and her eyes were trained solely on him.

"Samson, give me a minute, please," he told his assistant.

Samson began to argue, but Callan shot him a look that said there was no room for questions. "Fine. I'll be in the penthouse." Samson put his hands up in defeat.

Josie stepped closer the moment he was gone, but Callan grabbed her arm and pulled her around the corner to a small alcove where they could talk without being seen by any of the passing reporters—or, God forbid, Xavier Gray.

"What the hell are you doing here?" he hissed, keeping his voice as low as possible. If she was working for Gray and had set him up last night for some public relations stunt, he was going to lose his shit.

"Me?" She looked more angry than confused. Clearly she had some sort of understanding about the situation that he did not. "You didn't think to mention to me that *you* are Cal Walsh, the UFC fighter?"

He pushed his shoulders back. "Well, I certainly didn't realize I needed to," he replied, crossing his arms over his chest. "After all, I'm not the one who made up our list of rules."

"Those are rules for normal people." She slit her eyes into small lines, lifting her hand and wagging a finger at him. "Not famous UFC fighters competing against my boss."

"Your boss?" Callan clarified, trying to remember what she'd told him last night about her job.

She shrugged her shoulders. "Well, among other things."

So she was sleeping with him.

Fuck. He'd literally slept with the enemy.

"You know what?" he said, shaking his head. He couldn't believe he'd done something so stupid as to not even ask her if she was single first, let alone in a relationship with his biggest opponent ever. "Keep the dress. This—whatever *this* was—is over."

Her eyes widened, but they were filled with fire. "You don't get to tell *me* it's over," she replied, her voice lowering to a shrill whisper. "This never should have even started. And no one—I repeat, *no one*—can know about us. I cannot have tabloids finding this story out."

God, the fire in her spirit made his dick throb. He remembered that same passion from between the sheets and every memory of her perfect dark skin beneath his hands as he slid his tongue across every inch of her body.

Callan put out his hand, because frankly, he couldn't afford the scandal either. "Fine by me."

She rolled her eyes, ignoring his hand and storming away.

"Hey!" Callan called after her.

She glanced around them, making sure no one had heard him, and then quickly scurried back to him. "What?"

He gazed into her perfect green eyes—sparkling with a mixture of fear and irritation. "Tonight. My place. We tell no one."

Her mouth parted slightly, and her brows lifted in surprise. "What?"

He couldn't believe he'd said it either. But something about her . . . Fuck, he didn't want to stay away. Seeing her here, this close, yelling at him like she was in charge. He wanted nothing more than to remind her exactly who held the reins.

"We tell no one," he repeated. "No cameras. Just us. Just tonight. Get it out of our systems once and for all."

Her eyes narrowed again, but her tongue slid out across her lower lip. Her chest rose and fell faster as her breathing quickened. Oh yeah, he had her considering it.

"Who's to say I need to 'get you out of my system'?" She crossed her arms over her chest, lifting her chin slightly. Hell, she even looked intrigued.

Callan glanced around them for a moment, surveying how private an area they were in. Luckily, he saw no one. Stepping toward her, he forced her back farther into the alcove and slid his hand up her leg.

She panted, parting her legs slightly. It was like an automatic reaction to his touch, and he knew then and there that he had her . . . and that he wanted her. Sliding his hand across her panties, he felt her seeping through the silky fabric.

"You're wet just thinking about me," he said, growling against her ear as he leaned in closer.

He removed his hand, stepped backward, and brought his fingers to his lips and sucked on the tip, tasting her on his finger. Her eyes were sparkling with heat as she watched every move he made. "Tonight."

She bit the bottom corner of her lip, saying nothing in response.

He wasn't looking for a response, though. He'd already

gotten one. Instead, he walked away and left her waiting and wanting behind him.

He didn't look back. He never did when he made a decision, but this decision could cost him everything—or it could be exactly what he needed to get his concentration back and forget she ever existed in the first place.

Tonight would decide everything.

CHAPTER EIGHT

What the hell just happened? Josie blinked a few times, trying to reorient herself when she felt like everything in her world had just tipped upside down.

Seeing Callan step onto the stage and realizing he wasn't just Callan, a one-maybe-two-night stand that she'd never forget for the rest of her life. He was *the* Cal Walsh—her brother's opponent in next week's championship fight. He was the up-and-comer threatening to take down her family's empire and everything they'd worked for.

And this on top of their disastrous recent public relations.

Keeping her brother behaving and in line was a full-time job. One that she'd been slacking on—and because of that, her brother had recently found himself in some serious legal trouble.

To say her mother blamed her for it would be an understatement. But damn, he was a grown man. He could take care of himself. Still, there was nothing her brother could do that would make her mother mad at him. Everything was always Josie's fault, or someone else's fault, for tempting him to do the wrong thing. Her innocent baby boy was never to blame.

The family dynamics needed some work.

But what she definitely couldn't do was sleep with Callan again—like he'd proposed. *To get it out of our systems.* Honestly, he didn't know how true that was. She hadn't been able to stop thinking about their night together during the entire press junket. She was supposed to be feeding answers to her brother and helping him with the press, yet all she could do was stare across the stage at the gorgeous man she'd spent the night with, replaying it in her mind again . . . and again . . . and again.

It was just sex, sure. But it was the best sex she'd ever had in her entire freaking life.

And even then . . . was it just sex? It had felt like more, if she was really being honest with herself. She'd genuinely enjoyed the evening with him. Their misadventures in the desert, cooking breakfast at three o'clock in the morning—it had been like the longest and craziest date of her life.

Somehow, she wasn't entirely sure one night would be enough to get him out of her system. But it had to be. If she chose to go see him tonight.

That was a big *if*.

"Josie?" Xavier walked around the corner. "What are you doing here? The sound man said you turned your mic off. Everyone's headed to the Bellagio to celebrate. We're meeting the gang there and going to shoot a scene or two."

By that, he meant his groupies. There were at least twenty people following Xavier around at all times, and Josie barely knew them all by name. They came and went as casually as Xavier lived his life—different friends, different flings. He partied hard and expected the crowd he hung out with to do the same. Not everyone could keep up.

"I'm coming," she said, quickly trying to straighten out her dress and act like nothing had just happened. "I was just a little lost."

"In the MGM? How many times have we been here?"

"A lot, but you know . . ." Josie waved her hand. "Too many mimosas over breakfast."

Xavier laughed and clapped her on the back. "Hell yeah, you're coming out with us tonight. We're going to party it up big. Did you see me in there? This win is in the bag. Walsh was off his game big-time. Clearly I intimidate the hell out of him."

Her brother puffed out his chest with pride.

Josie just nodded, even though she could probably guess why Callan had been a little off today. It wasn't that noticeable, truthfully, but Xavier was trained to look for weaknesses, and when Callan had hesitated as they'd first walked in, Xavier had pounced on it. She'd seen the moment it had happened. Confidence built in her brother, and here she was finding herself confused as to who she was hoping would win.

Maybe Callan was right. Maybe that was *exactly* why they needed to get out of each other's systems. Even after only one night together, they'd clearly muddied each other's minds.

"I can't go out tonight," she said. "Maybe tomorrow."

"No." Xavier shook his head. "We're going out tonight. I'll send the stylist to your place this afternoon with a couple of choice outfits. We all need to look our best. Keep our image as high as we can right now."

She bit the corner of her lip. "Okay."

There was no other choice. No other option when it came to her brother and his demands.

Maybe this was fate's way of deciding for her.

Callan Walsh was off-limits.

CHAPTER NINE

"What do you mean 'take the evening off'?" Samson squinted his eyes at Callan, as if he was trying to see through his bullshit. "We have a fight in five days, and you want to just . . . take a personal day?"

"I've been working all day," Callan pointed out. "I'm only taking tonight off to relax and unwind. It's been a long day. You should do the same."

Samson looked confused, his brows pinched together. "You haven't given me an evening off in the year I've worked for you. Something's going on." His eyes widened, and he clapped his hands together. "Oh, my God, am I being fired? I'm getting married in less than two months, Cal. How are Elliott and I supposed to pay for all of that without me working?"

Elliott, Samson's soon-to-be husband, was his favorite topic to bring up no matter what the conversation. Callan swore the two were perfect for each other, because all they did was fawn over one another. It was sickening to watch sometimes because it was so mushy. Callan was not the ooey-gooey, lovey-dovey type. He had strict rules and boundaries, and he never let a woman cross them.

But he'd never been in love before, so what did he really know?

It wasn't that he didn't want to find love or settle down eventually. It just wasn't part of the plan at the moment. He'd been working toward being a championship UFC fighter for years, only finally exploding publicly about a year ago. People called him an overnight success, but the truth was, a ton of effort was behind that success.

That was the funny thing about overnight success—people always wanted to know his secret, but it was just a decade of hard work and determination.

"No one's getting fired," Callan assured his assistant. "I just want some time to myself. Is that really so weird?"

"Considering that you're basically a loner who likes to spend all his time by himself?" Samson shook his head. "No, it's not that weird. All right. I'll see you first thing in the morning, then. Remember to post at least three tweets tonight! We need to up your social media game!"

Callan nodded, ushering him out the door of the penthouse hotel suite he'd be calling home for at least the next week before traveling back to Los Angeles. Finally alone, he went to the bedroom to retrieve his phone and pulled up Josie's contact information. They'd exchanged numbers last night, and he wanted to find out what time she'd be here so he could have a repeat performance—and more.

What's your ETA?

He pressed Send and waited for the three bubbles to appear to show she was writing back. After a minute of silence, he gave up and put his phone back down. He needed a shower before she got here anyway, so he might as well knock that out of the way.

He stripped himself of his clothes and walked to the shower, turning on the water once he reached it. He tried not to think about the fact that the last person to shower in here had been Josie. The very image of her wet, naked body dripping with water flashed in front of his eyes, and his cock hardened in response.

Stepping under the warm stream of water, he gripped his shaft with one hand and pumped slowly as he thought of her. Perfect, kissable nipples that budded beneath his tongue, begging for more attention. An ass he could grip with both hands and feel the delicious weight in his palms. Eyes that pierced straight through him and sent shivers across his entire body.

Everything about her was sensual and warm.

He stopped pumping before he came, wanting to save his orgasms for later. He wanted her.

A ping sounded from the other room, and he knew he'd received a text message. Quickly rushing through the rest of his shower, he finished cleaning himself and then turned off the water. He reached for a towel and wrapped it around his body as he stepped out and headed for the bedroom. Picking up the phone, he scrolled to his text messages.

Can't tonight.

That was her entire response. No explanation. No apologies. Nothing but rejection.

He didn't respond at first, leaving her simply on read status.

Admittedly, he wasn't used to rejection, and he certainly wasn't used to being told no. It wasn't a pleasant feeling, and he decided then and there that he wasn't going to accept it. She wanted to come over tonight as badly as he wanted her to—he knew that from their exchange earlier today. She'd been practically panting, begging for him to take her right then and there in the hotel conference room hallway.

Taking the chance, he texted back with the passcode for the elevator to get to the penthouse and told her he'd leave the front door unlocked. And then added:

Come when you're free later.

She responded almost immediately.

Maybe.

CHAPTER TEN

"Don't you think you've had enough?" Josie took the shot glass out of Xavier's hand and emptied its contents into a nearby plant. Cameras were pointed right at her, but she didn't even see them anymore. She was so used to living her life on camera that it was easy to pretend they weren't even watching. "I think it's time we head home."

"Killjoy." Xavier slurred his words, leaning an arm across his sister's shoulder as he pointed to the rest of his crew. "You all want to keep going, right?"

A few random girls with thigh-high boots and miniskirts were clinging to him like molasses, and they all chimed in with their agreement, begging him to stay.

"I could head back," said Tyson, one of his friends and crew members who always traveled with them. "Josie, you taking Xavier home?"

She nodded. "I've got him."

"I've got myself," Xavier argued, wagging his finger in her face. "I'm a mother fucking badass, and we're going to tear. This. Bitch. Up!"

He was yelling now, and the crowd at the club around them was getting hyped up with him, cheering him on. It only fed into his mood—and his ego—encouraging him to get even more dramatic and put on more of a show.

Hell, that was their whole life. Xavier putting on a show for the world.

It was what he did, and now it was what she was doing alongside him.

"It's almost one o'clock in the morning," Josie argued, trying to stifle a yawn she felt coming on at the very mention of the late hour. "Time to head back to the hotel."

"Jos, just because you don't have any fun doesn't mean I can't have fun," Xavier babbled.

She huffed. "I have plenty of fun."

He laughed. "Bullshit. You've got a stick so far up your ass, you don't know how to stand on your own two feet without it."

"Xav, seriously. It's time to go." He was becoming belligerent, and this was the part of the evening she hated most. He always got like this and acted like an asshole, but normally it wasn't directed at her.

"And you know what else?" Xavier continued on. "You're not even that pretty. Guys at the gym are always asking about you, and I'm like... why? What the hell do they see in my mouse of a sister? You're only famous because of me."

She swallowed hard, trying not to let tears sting her eyes, like they were threatening to.

"I'm going to ask you one last time to come back to the hotel, or I'm going to freaking leave you here," she ground out, barely able to open her clenched jaw. "Now."

"Fuck. Off." Xavier stumbled over to one of the random groupie girls and started making out with her. The cameras turned to pan in her direction, wanting to get her reaction to his comments.

She slammed her glass down on the table between them, making a loud *thunk*. That was it. She was leaving.

God, sometimes she hated Vegas, and she hated this fucking reality television show.

"He's all yours, T," she told Tyson before handing her microphone to a cameraman and walking straight out of the club.

The moment she stepped onto the sidewalk, the cool Las Vegas night air hit her, and tears welled in her eyes. She tried to hold them back, but they flowed down her cheeks anyway.

Glancing down at her phone, she scrolled back to her text messages with Callan. It'd been hours since he'd last texted her that he still wanted to see her tonight. She was sure he was already asleep, having given up entirely on her.

But maybe he wasn't?

Pulling open the Lyft app so she could remain private, she called a car to take her back to the MGM. She didn't need her personal driver telling anyone where she was going.

Within twenty minutes, she was back in the hotel lobby, heading toward the elevators. She wasn't entirely convinced about what she was going to do, but she had no plans to turn back now.

Punching in the code he gave her for the penthouse, she was soon on her way up to his floor. Sure enough, his front door was unlocked just like he'd said it would be. The living room she had been in just under twenty-fours ago was now dark, with one lone light on in the corner.

She closed the door behind her and locked it, sliding off her shoes so she could tiptoe quietly to the bedroom. When she opened the door to the bedroom, it cast a lighted path across the room and the bed. Callan's bare abs were draped in the light, as he was lying on his back across the bed, but the rest of him was covered in darkness.

Relief flooded her at the sight of him—a crazy feeling for someone she barely knew, but what she did know was that she needed him right now.

After slipping out of her dress, she tossed it over a chair and then slid into bed next to him, only wearing her bra and panties. She curled into his side but didn't wake him.

He stirred and threw an arm around her, wrapping his body around hers. "Mmm, I knew you'd come."

"I said maybe," she teased, trying to remain lighthearted, even though she felt like the weight of the world was sitting on her chest.

Callan buried his face in her neck, kissing her gently and holding her even tighter against him. "Is everything okay?" he asked. "I wasn't expecting an early morning wakeup call."

She nodded, but a lump began to form in her throat.

"Josie?" Callan wasn't buying her simple head nod. "What's wrong?"

He lifted her up and turned her around to face him, wrapping his arms tighter around her once again.

"Nothing," she insisted, though nothing about her tone sounded genuine.

Tears began to collect on her lashes, threatening to spill sideways onto the mattress beneath them.

"You're crying," he said, barely above a whisper, as he touched her cheek with the pad of his thumb. He wiped at the tear that slid down her nose. "What's wrong?"

"I didn't come here to tell you my life problems," she said, swallowing hard and trying to take a deep breath. "I just needed some company."

"Well, lucky for you, we offer extra services besides just amazing sex here," he teased, kissing her cheek. "I've heard our listening package is rated quite high."

She chuckled, sniffing back her tears at his humor.

"I just think I'm ready to quit some days," she admitted. "Like today. I'm so, so close to quitting the show, and then I just... I can't."

"Why can't you?" he asked. "Your boyfriend won't let you?"

"Boyfriend?" Josie's brows pinched together as she tried to figure out what he was talking about. "I'm not dating anyone."

"You're not dating Xavier Gray?" he asked, looking surprised.

Josie grimaced, nausea entering her psyche at the thought. "My brother? Hell, I fucking hope not."

"You're his sister?" Callan clarified. He must have remembered her having said she worked for her brother. Her guess was he'd assumed that her brother was in management for Gray—not Gray himself. To be fair, she and her brother looked nothing alike. "And you're his assistant. Okay. I got it now. That makes more sense."

"Did you really think I would have come here last night if I had a boyfriend?" That was a little insulting. She'd never cheated on anyone and wasn't the type to be even interested in that.

"No," he countered. "That's why it was confusing. It didn't match the person I knew. Then again... I've only known you for one day."

Strange how comfortable one could get with someone in a day.

They had buried a body together, so there was that.

"That's kind of weird, isn't it?" Josie asked him, curling tighter into his chest.

He looked down at her. "That we've only known each other for one day?"

She nodded. "It feels like longer. It feels ..."

"Comfortable," he finished for her.

She hadn't been sure what word she was going to use, but when he said that, she knew he was right. Things were somehow comfortable between the two of them, as if they just ... fit. She'd never felt that type of connection with someone before, and it was freaking terrifying to her that she was feeling it now. Not only did she have no idea if he was feeling the same depth of feelings she was, but this also couldn't work.

He was still the enemy.

She couldn't cross that line.

Although, here she was, in bed with the enemy ... quite literally.

Callan leaned down and placed a kiss on her lips, soft and inviting. She suddenly wanted more, wanted him, wanted to forget this night had ever happened and wash it away with the pleasure only he could bring her. Wrapping her arms around his neck, she deepened their kiss and pulled him to her as tight as she could.

"Mmm," he moaned against her lips, reaching down and sliding her panties off.

He pressed her back into the mattress, climbing over her as he positioned himself between her legs. Moving against her slick entrance, he slid inside her with one long thrust. His mouth captured hers, and they kissed as he pumped in and out until they were both shaking and trembling as their orgasms passed through them. He buried himself deeper, releasing.

It crossed her mind for a moment that they hadn't used a condom, but she pushed the thought aside.

Collapsing onto the mattress next to her, he pulled her body against his. "You're amazing, Jos, and you deserve to be happy in your job and in your life."

She was still panting as she came down from her high, so she didn't respond, but she did squeeze him tighter against her, loving the feel of his body wrapped around hers. Every part of her knew he was right. What was she doing still working for her brother or doing that show? Why was she putting up with his shit day in and day out?

Shouldn't her happiness come first? Or did family *always* trump that?

Josie closed her eyes, drifting off to sleep as she mulled over what to do with her life and who she wanted to be.

His whisper soft against her ear was the last thing she heard. "Good night, little one."

CHAPTER ELEVEN

Josie awoke leisurely late the next morning, not even bothering to turn on her phone and check the messages she was sure she'd missed. She'd definitely missed call time for filming, but she didn't care.

Turning over in bed, she realized she was alone.

"Callan?" she called out, sitting up as she pulled the sheets up over her chest. Glancing around, she spied a note on the bedside table.

Have to go to an event. Didn't want to wake you.
Be naked when I get back.

She glanced at the clock. It was almost lunchtime. Finding her phone, she turned it on and waited as all the missed messages and notifications downloaded. Without bothering to check what her brother had said, she shot Xavier and the producers a quick text.

Taking the day off today. Not feeling well.

She could see the three bubbles appear immediately under her text, showing that her brother was texting her right back, but she didn't want to see what he said. She turned her phone back off entirely and lay back on the mattress.

Was she being selfish taking a day off filming right before

a huge fight? Ironically, with the man she was sleeping with.

Josie took a deep breath and reminded herself that Xavier had two other perfectly good assistants and that she worked her ass off for him. Hell, she was on call twenty-four-seven and often up in the middle of the night caring for his drunk ass.

It was okay to take a break.

A much-needed one, at that.

Her stomach growled, and she realized it had been a while since she'd eaten anything. After climbing out of bed, she headed for the kitchen and began rummaging through the fridge to see what she could find. It was fully stocked, and she decided to have a bacon, lettuce, and tomato sandwich for lunch.

Pulling out all the ingredients for the BLT, Josie got to work and decided to prepare an extra one in case Callan came back soon.

Turned out, she was right on time.

"Am I smelling bacon right now?" She heard him before she saw him, but when he rounded the corner, he looked like a kid with cake. "I'm an absolute sucker for bacon."

"Guess it's a good thing I made you a BLT," she said, cutting his sandwich in half and sliding the plate toward him. She cut hers in half next and then took a big bite.

"Can I just hire you to be my personal chef?" he teased, finishing the first half of his sandwich in record time. "I could eat your food all day long."

She laughed, although that did sound like a dream gig. If only she wasn't going back to her real life after this. "Where did you go off to this morning?" she asked.

"Media training," he replied, already biting into the last half of his sandwich. "They're really trying to up my social media image and all that shit." He paused, looking at her closely. "Sorry. I shouldn't be talking about this stuff with you. It puts you in a weird position."

She shrugged her shoulders. He wasn't wrong, and yet, she still wanted to hear about his life. Fuck. That was *too* comfortable. She needed to set some boundaries.

"What do you have going on today?" he asked, finishing his sandwich.

"I took the day off."

He lifted one brow. "Really? No cameras?"

"New deal and terms," she proposed. "I was thinking I'd just stay here and hide out for a little. Then tomorrow, I'll go back to my real life, and you—you go back to being the enemy."

"I agree to your terms," he replied almost instantly, as if he didn't even have to think about it. "But I will be in and out a lot today because of work. I want you, however, to enjoy the day here. Order a massage. Pedicure. Go to the spa. Whatever. My treat."

Relief eased the tension in her shoulders as she looked at him for a moment, quietly contemplating.

"What?" he asked, clearly noticing her silence.

She shook her head. "I just . . . I just don't understand why you'd do all that for me. I'm literally the enemy, and we've only known each other for two days."

Callan grinned. "Still—no one else I'd rather bury a body with."

Josie laughed, smacking him lightly on the chest. "Poor Sienna. I hope she's okay."

"You've lost your mind," he teased, pulling her closer to him and kissing her temple. Leaning down, he found her lips, and she parted slightly as his mouth covered hers. When she started pulling him toward the bedroom, he gently slapped her ass. "I swear I'm going to need a day off after I'm done with you."

She wiggled her butt as she glanced back over her shoulder. "There's always tomorrow."

Except, for them, there wasn't. And her heart ached at the reminder.

CHAPTER TWELVE

Despite the fact that he'd had to work part of the day yesterday, Callan had still managed to spend a great deal of time with Josie holed away in his penthouse. They'd watched movies, gotten a couple's massage, and had more sex than he could almost physically handle. But waking up the next morning, all of that seemed to be erased.

He found his bed to be empty, the sheets cold. She must have been gone for a while.

"Josie?" he called out around the penthouse, standing up and going in search of her. He found himself hoping that she was in the kitchen, cooking them breakfast like she had been the last few times he'd found her.

But no . . . the penthouse was empty, and he knew that was probably for the best.

They'd spent their time together, and now it was over. Now he could focus on what he needed to be focused on—work, training, fighting.

She had been a distraction, one that could have cost him the fight.

But he was doubling down now.

Callan lifted his phone to his ear after dialing his assistant's phone number. "Samson? What's on the itinerary today?"

"Gym from nine to twelve, and then we have lunch with the reporter from the *LA Times* doing the spread on you," Samson began to rattle off the schedule. "This afternoon is the *People* magazine photo shoot with you and Gray. Tonight is dinner with some corporate bigwigs from the UFC and then an after-dinner strategy session with Ferguson."

Callan took a deep breath and blew it out. "All right. Let's fucking do it. Meet me at the gym at quarter to twelve."

"Got it, boss."

"Also, place my lunch order at Niro's."

"Steak and pommes frites? Well done?" Samson asked.

Callan laughed and shook his head. "Medium, you psycho."

"I'll convert you to well-done steaks one day," Samson joked and then hung up.

Callan grabbed some workout clothes, shoved them into his bag, and then headed down to the UFC training center.

"Hey, Walsh," Ferguson, his trainer, said as he entered the center. "Ready to hop in the cage?"

Callan nodded, passing him and heading straight for the locker rooms. "I'll be right out."

In the locker rooms, he paused after he finished changing and looked at himself in the mirror. He had bags under his eyes that normally weren't there. Probably from the lack of sleep the last few days. He definitely needed to get more sleep this coming week if he was going to get proper workouts in.

There was a bite mark on his shoulder, and he smiled, remembering where it came from. Josie was wild in bed, and he'd loved every second of it.

Five minutes later, he was warming up on the sandbags. With each punch, he felt himself getting back into the groove of things. Being in the gym and training was his way of relaxing and centering himself, and there was nothing he liked better than the feeling of his muscles being pushed to their limits.

After a quick warm-up, he began sparring with Ferguson in the main cage—the center octagon at the training facility.

"You're off your game today, Cal," his trainer pointed out after he was able to land a punch square in Cal's shoulder that he hadn't blocked in time.

Callan shook it off and took a few deep breaths, trying to re-energize himself. "I know. I'm just tired. I need more sleep."

"Remember what we have going for us that your opponent doesn't?" Ferguson asked.

"Aside from not being a fucking drunk who drives his car into mothers and children?"

Xavier Gray was an asshole, and Callan still couldn't believe he was related to Josie. She seemed nothing like him in the least, and she also didn't seem like the type to tolerate his shitty behavior. How could she work for him?

She was so much more talented than to be an assistant for the likes of him. That was what he couldn't figure out. Why was she wasting her time at this dead-end job she wasn't passionate about when she had real talents, like cooking, that she could utilize?

"Cal. Focus. Earth to Cal!" Ferguson snapped his fingers in front of Callan's face. "Are you even paying attention to me?"

Callan realized that Ferguson had been talking to him for the last few minutes and he'd been completely tuning him out. "What?"

"I'm only going to say this one time, so you better listen up." Ferguson stepped closer to him, irritation coursing through his knit brows and clenched jaw. "If you lose this fight, everything you've worked for over the last ten years is over. This is your first, and maybe only, chance to be named a champion, to receive the recognition in this field that you've been working toward. Gray? He's already established. He has enough belts on his wall to last him the rest of his life. Winning this fight would just be another one in the bucket for him. But for you? This is your big break, Cal."

Callan nodded his head, more than understanding what his trainer was telling him. He had worked his way up the circuit over the last few years, but he had yet to compete in any major championships or challenges. Sure, he was undefeated, but that meant nothing if you'd only been playing in the minor leagues.

This was his opportunity to kick his career up into the majors. This was his opportunity to win his first championship—his first belt.

"So whatever has you distracted," Ferguson continued, "whatever has you not sleeping—fix it now. Get it out of your fucking life. You've worked too hard to let something trip you up at the finish line."

"Got it." Callan rubbed his hands through his hair and tied it up into a ponytail. "It's already gone. I'm focused."

Ferguson lifted one brow as if he didn't entirely believe him. "I'll see you tonight for our strategy session. Get in a good workout before the photo shoot this afternoon. This is your second chance to intimidate Gray and get into his head. Remind him who's going to kick his ass in that cage."

Callan understood. As much time as he spent training and working out, a good portion of winning was in mental fortitude. Showing himself to be unshakable in front of his opponent in the days leading up to a fight was all part of the mental warfare needed to win.

He'd nearly fucked that up at the press junket, being unnerved by Josie's presence, but he wasn't going to let that happen this time. He was going to show Gray exactly how strong he was and how he never backed down from a fight.

CHAPTER THIRTEEN

It was one thing knowing that Callan was going to be at the photo shoot. Josie had been prepared for that. It was a joint photo shoot between both opponents, as they were both part of a feature on the hottest UFC fighters.

But knowing he was going to be there and that she'd have to ignore him was entirely different than actually being there in person and watching him get the most sensual rubdown she'd ever seen in a public setting. It was clearly a type of karmic torture for something horrible she'd done in a past life.

The woman spreading oil on Callan's body had big blond hair, giant tits that she had to have paid for, and an ass that she'd jammed into the shortest shorts possible.

And she was enjoying every second of her job.

Josie was too far away to hear what they were talking about, since she was over by her brother, who was getting the same thing from another giant-titted blonde. But she could see the woman whispering to Callan every few moments, and then he'd laugh or say something back, and every single smile on his face was like a cheese grater running over her heart.

She wanted to slap the smile off his face and remind him exactly whose legs he'd been between less than twenty-four hours ago.

Okay, to be fair, he wasn't fucking the woman right in front of her. Hell, he probably wasn't even really flirting. But that damn oily goddess was flirting. She was flirting within an inch of her life. The way she squeezed her arms together in front of her to push up her boobs even closer to Callan's face . . . or the way she kept dropping the oil bottle and having to turn around and pick it up, conveniently putting her ass on display. Josie wasn't an amateur. She could tell a hustler from a mile away, and this woman was all about that groupie—

"Josie, for Christ's sake," Shondra Gray interrupted her thoughts, waving her hands in front of Josie's face. "Have you even heard a word I've said?"

She realized she hadn't even noticed her mother was talking until just this minute. "Uh, can you repeat that last part for me? I got the rest," she lied.

"I was saying that we should get some dinner tonight. Just the two of us." Shondra crossed her arms over her chest, eyeing her daughter carefully. "Xav's got strategy sessions after this, and it would be nice to just do something—you and I."

"Sure," Josie agreed. "Let's do it. Off camera?"

"No, we'll film the dinner. But in the meantime"— Shondra lowered her voice and leaned in—"you realize you're eye-fucking the competition, right? The cameras can see you."

Josie nearly jumped ten feet in the air. "What?"

"I didn't stutter," her mother replied, lifting one brow in the air as she surveyed Josie's expression.

From the heat searing her face, she could just imagine how red she must've been. "I wasn't."

"It's fine with me. Just don't let your brother see." Shondra glanced over to where Xavier was openly flirting with the woman oiling him up. "I already have enough to worry about with your brother."

She nodded but didn't respond to her mother's comment. Instead, she decided to change the subject. "Is he done being mad at me yet?"

"Xav?" Shondra shrugged. "He'll get over your day off, but that doesn't make what you did okay. We've got to stay focused right now, honey. There's no time for a sick day right now."

"I'm feeling a lot better today." Josie kept up the pretense of her lie, reassuring her mother.

She began to realize that she was lying a lot. It seemed to roll easily off her tongue, and that worried her. It was as if she'd gotten used to living an inauthentic life, and it didn't even faze her anymore to go against her own value system.

"Good. I have someone I want you to meet." Shondra motioned across the room to a man in a suit who was discussing something heated with the photographer. "Follow me."

Like the dutiful daughter, Josie followed her mother over to the two men.

"Jamie, have you met my daughter?" Shondra asked, interrupting the man's conversation with the photographer.

Dark eyes turned up to look at her, and a smile cast across his face as he reached a hand out. "I don't believe I've had the pleasure."

Josie took his hand, shaking it. "Josie Gray. I'm Xavier's assistant and younger sister."

He did a double take, glancing between Xavier and her. "You two look nothing alike," he remarked.

"Thank God," Josie said with a laugh, poking fun at her brother.

Jamie's grin doubled, and he chuckled. "I'm Jamie Sessions, head producer of Lion Head Studios."

"Oh." That was the name of the studio that had just recently purchased their show and was marketing them to *E! News*. "It's great to meet you."

"We'd like to talk to you about upping your role in the

show," Jamie continued, pulling her and her mother aside slightly. "We have a proposal for you."

"What kind of proposal?" her mother asked, always in manager mode.

Josie was immediately skeptical because there was no doubt whatever the proposal was, it was first and foremost good for the studio and likely to be shitty for her.

"An episode where you're the frontrunner." Jamie crossed his arms over his chest. "Poll numbers make it clear—fans are interested in you. Viewership is going down for the show in general, but we think getting a younger audience invested in you, Josie Gray, will bring in a whole new fan base. After all, you have nearly two million Instagram followers."

She shrugged, not thinking that much about her social media platform. She posted pictures and people liked them. It wasn't that difficult, but he was right. People did seem fascinated with her life and wanted to know what she was doing every day.

"So . . . what would the episode be about?"

Jamie glanced across the room. "Have you ever met Cal Walsh?"

Josie kept her face as straight as possible. "Not personally, no."

Another lie. So easy.

"We want you to go on a date with him." Jamie grinned like it was the smartest thing he'd ever said and was impressed with himself. "We've talked to his manager, and they're going to pose the idea to him as well."

She coughed, trying to stop herself from laughing, because if that wasn't the funniest twist of events, she didn't know what was.

"And you can't tell your brother about it," Jamie said. "The whole point will be that it's behind his back. That's the story we're going to run with."

Josie looked at her mother, who seemed to be eating up this story line along with Jamie. "Ma, you're okay with this?"

After all, her mother had just reamed her out about the competition a minute ago.

Her mother paused for a moment. "I think it's one dinner. Harmless. As long as everyone is on their best behavior."

She got the subtle dig—a reminder to never do anything to screw the family.

"So go get your mic on, because we're going to stage the scene between the two of you as soon as Xavier finishes shooting and leaves," Sessions finished explaining and then handed her a call sheet with instructions.

Sure, she was a reality television star, but that didn't mean all their shows were reality. Staged and scripted was a more accurate version of their reality. Josie wondered if that was where she got lying so easily from—living a fake version of her life day in and day out.

"Ma, I don't know about this..." Josie cautioned her mother, seeing the potential pitfalls. "Don't you think it's too much of a conflict?"

Shondra shook her head. "I actually think this could be great for Xav," she explained. "If you can keep Walsh distracted for a few days, maybe even get him to fall in love, then Xav could run him over in the ring."

"Ma!" Josie's eyes widened. "I'm not going to trick some guy just so Xav can get a win."

Her mother cut her eyes to her. "I didn't say go have sex with him," she clarified. "Just play with his head a little. Get him off his game. You wouldn't do this for family? For your brother?"

Josie groaned internally at the reminder. *Fuck this family.*

Producers came over and set up her mic pack around her waist under her clothes and then prepped her with a few dialogue lines that they really wanted her to hit. Josie put the conversation with her mother out of her head and tried to focus on the show. She filmed a few behind-the-scenes clips and interviews and then talked with producers about how the rest of the show would go with Callan.

It was all business and fake as hell. Just the way she lived her life.

An hour later, Xavier had finished shooting and was on his way to his next event, while Callan still lingered.

Josie pulled out her phone and fired off a quick text to Callan.

Are we really doing this?

If that's what you want.

As if she had a say in any of this. Though, to be truthful for once, she was actually looking forward to the idea of a formal date with Callan. It would be nice to actually be seen in public and spend time with one another outside of his penthouse. The fact was, she really liked the guy.

"Josie, right?" Callan approached her as she was packing a bag of outfit choices her brother had brought with him for the photo shoot.

She glanced up at him as he moved in. Thick brown hair in waves around his face, tattoos rippling against his skin as he stood shirtless in front of her. God, she couldn't help but remember how amazing his body had felt pressed against her in bed not so long ago. He smoldered when he moved, and there was no doubt he had the attention of every woman in the room.

But he was here. With her.

Nerves fluttered in her stomach, which was odd because she knew exactly what was going to happen. She'd already read the script. *Why am I nervous?*

"Yes," she replied, extending a hand to him as if they were just meeting for the first time. "And you're Callan Walsh."

He blushed slightly—actually blushed. It was rather adorable. "That's me."

"How can I help you, Mr. Walsh?" she asked, tucking the rest of her brother's clothes into the suitcase and zipping it up. "I'm about to head out."

Callan kicked at the ground lightly where he was standing, seeming to try to find his words. A camera crew surrounded them, their lenses focused on them for a tight shot. Josie wondered if Callan had ever been filmed like this before, and maybe nerves were getting the better of him.

But then he looked up at her—kind eyes with slight crinkles in the corners—and a smile overtook his expression. He was pandering to the cameras.

She had to control her lips from slipping into a grin, keeping a thin line to her mouth. *What a natural.*

"I couldn't help but notice you throughout the photo shoot," he said, leaning in a little closer. "I was wondering if maybe you wanted to grab dinner tonight? Drinks?"

Josie stood up straight and faced him, lifting one brow as she took him in. "Drinks, huh?"

"Could be fun." He winked at her. Actually winked. My God, the man was made for television. "It can be our little secret."

"If my brother found out…" she warned, hitting the talking points in the script she'd been given.

Callan moved closer, running his hand down her arm in a gentle caress. "I won't tell if you don't tell."

He then stepped back and gave her a wide grin. "Tonight. Seven o'clock. Niro's."

Niro's was one of her favorite restaurants and incredibly hard to get into. It was on the strip and had a reservation list tighter than Fort Knox.

"Okay," she said simply, lifting the suitcase and making her way toward the exit.

She could feel his eyes on her as she walked away, and she loved every second of it.

Tonight might be a fake date, but her excitement was very real.

CHAPTER FOURTEEN

"When's the last time you've even been on a date?" Samson asked Callan, handing him a shirt he'd just picked up from the dry cleaners.

Callan shrugged. He wasn't about to reveal the truth to his assistant, because as much as he trusted the guy, he also knew his tendency to be a bit loose-lipped when it came to gossip. "It's been a while," he said simply. "Dating hasn't really been a priority of mine."

Samson just nodded. "Well, this shirt works perfectly on you. Just remember to wine and dine her. You really want her to like you for the show. It's important for your image that you come across as the good guy."

"I still can't believe you convinced me to do this." Callan pulled on his shirt and examined himself in the mirror. "I've never been on a reality television show before."

"We're trying to make you famous in more than just the UFC market, Cal," Samson reminded him. "This show will boost your popularity and expose you to an entirely new audience."

He understood, but that still didn't mean he wasn't reluctant. When he'd first figured out that Josie was a reality television star, he'd been a bit reticent to continue things with her, especially considering his own career path and how that might affect him. He was already worried enough that his entanglement with her would be a distraction from the fight in a few days.

He hadn't thought of it as a positive, however. Samson took one look at it and saw dollar signs.

"You were meant to be on television," Samson assured him. "You were meant to be a star."

Callan didn't necessarily agree, but he wasn't about to argue with the facts—he needed more publicity to expand his career, and Josie had an entire platform of untapped potential fans. It was a win-win.

"Want me to come with you for the filming?" Samson asked, handing him his jacket and tie as they headed for the door in preparation to leave for the restaurant.

"And chaperone my date?" Callan shook his head. "I think I'll be fine on my own."

"I'll text you halfway through to see how it's going," Samson compromised.

Thirty minutes later, his driver was pulling up in front of Niro's, where he saw a camera crew already waiting for him outside.

"Walsh," a tall man with curly brown hair called out to him as he stepped out of the car. He extended his hand and shook the man's hand. "Jamie Sessions. Ready to do this? The sound man is going to get a mic on you, and then I'll go over a few talking points."

"Is Josie already here?" Callan asked the producer.

Jamie shook his head. "She's meeting with my assistant producer and going over her talking points now. She'll be here in about ten minutes."

They set him up with a mic pack under his shirt, and Jamie gave him some suggestions of things to go over during dinner that they wanted to film. It was all very . . . clinical and not at all what he was expecting for his first date with Josie. He found himself a little disappointed.

When the camera crew was finally ready, they began filming just as Josie's car pulled up to the curb. Callan realized it must have been timed like that.

"Hey there," he greeted her, opening the car door for her and offering her his hand.

She accepted it and climbed out of the car, stepping onto the sidewalk. "Hi."

"Ready for this?" he asked, feeling some nerves as the cameras pointed in his face.

Josie didn't even seem to notice the camera crew around her. "I've been looking forward to this all day."

They headed into the restaurant together and were immediately seated. A waiter came and brought them drinks and appetizers that they hadn't even ordered but apparently production had set up ahead of time. Everything was streamlined and simple, and he realized he didn't have to think about a thing except Josie.

"Is it always like this for you?" he asked.

Josie tilted her head to the side. "Like what?"

"Your life. On camera. Is it always so structured? So scripted?" He knew he wasn't supposed to talk about filming because that was considered breaking the fourth wall, but they'd already exhausted all their talking points over appetizers, and he was tired of the aimless chit chat just for the cameras' sake.

"It's the job." A sadness crept over Josie's expression, her brows knitted together as she seemed to think about his question. "It's kind of sad ... isn't it?"

He didn't say anything. It didn't seem like she really wanted a response. It was more like she was contemplating out loud.

"I guess I've just gotten so used to it . . . the lack of privacy, the cameras, the mechanics of it all." Josie picked up her wineglass and took a sip. "It's been our life for years. Well, my brother's life. We're just all along for the ride."

"Tell me about your dreams," he prompted. "What did you want before all of this happened?"

"I've been trying to land a job in a kitchen for over a year now. I wanted to be a sous chef, but I'd take anything at this point," she admitted. He knew she loved to cook, but he couldn't say that without revealing they already knew one another, so he stayed quiet. "Everywhere I apply either doesn't get back to me or flat out rejects me."

He scrunched his brows together. "Really? Do they say why?"

She shook her head. "I usually can't even get a call back. My guess is that they don't want to be associated with the show . . . or with my brother. With everything that's happened over the last two years with his partying . . . well, we've all taken the hit."

That didn't seem fair.

"I don't know if this is helpful or not, but I'm friends with Michael Rockport," Callan suggested with a small shrug.

Her eyes seemed to bug out of her head. "The owner of this place? Niro's? And like ten other restaurants around the country? The star of *Rock the Kitchen* on the Food Network?"

Callan nodded. "He's a big UFC fan. Arranged a meet-and-greet after one of my fights, and we just hit it off."

"No wonder you got us in here so easily." She clucked her tongue. "I was wondering how production had managed to pull that off."

"It's one of my favorite places when I come to Vegas,"

Callan admitted. "Mike should step out and see us at some point. He knows I'm here."

She gripped the table, her knuckles turning white. "What? I will be *meeting* Michael Rockport?"

Callan chuckled lightly, amused at the childlike innocence with which she spoke. "If you want, sure."

"Shut up!" She reached out and smacked him on the shoulder. "You could have led with that, you know?"

Sure enough, ten minutes later, as they were scanning the dessert menu, a tall bald man with deep-blue eyes walked over to them. He was wearing a chef's coat and didn't look a day over thirty-five thanks to the magic of plastic surgery.

"Walsh!" Michael greeted him with a big hug as Callan stood up to embrace his friend.

"Good to see you, Mike," he replied.

"Tell me—are you a lock to win on Saturday?" Mike asked. "I have front-row tickets and a shit ton of cash bet on this fight. Should I double down?"

"Triple down," Callan kidded. "I'm going to kick Gray's ass around that cage like a damn doll."

Josie coughed, clearly trying to get his attention.

"Mike, this is actually Gray's younger sister, Josie," Callan said, introducing her to his friend.

She eagerly shook the man's hand. "It's such a pleasure to meet you, Mr. Rockport."

"The pleasure is all mine, though I have to admit, I'm not betting on your brother to win Saturday." Michael laughed, and his stomach shook like a bowl of jelly with the movement.

Josie didn't seem to care one bit.

They chatted for a little while longer until the waiter brought some dessert out and Michael had to excuse himself back to the kitchen.

"That was amazing," Josie said, taking his hand across the table. "Thank you for indulging my fan-girl side."

Callan shrugged like it was no big deal. "I'm going to run to the bathroom really quick. I'll be right back."

She nodded and took a bite of the chocolate cake they'd ordered.

He excused himself and headed in the direction of the bathrooms, but when he was out of view of Josie, he bee-lined straight for the kitchen instead.

"Hey, Mike," Callan called into the kitchen, waving over his friend. "Let me chat with you really quickly."

"What's up?" The chef came over to greet him.

"My girl over there, Josie. She's an amazing chef. She can cook—"

Michael shook his head. "Before you ask me to give her a job or something like that, I have to tell you something."

He paused. "What?"

"She's been blacklisted." Michael crossed his arms over his chest. "I know who she is, and her brother has made it very clear to everyone in Las Vegas that if they hire her, they are going to face his wrath. No one on the strip is going to take that chance."

Callan blinked twice, trying to register what his friend was saying. "Are you serious?"

Michael nodded. "I just can't risk it, man. Best of luck."

They shook hands, and Michael headed back into the kitchen.

He glanced back toward where Josie was sitting and tried to decide how to handle this. Did he tell her? Did he throw her brother under the bus like that? He wasn't sure how she'd handle the news or whether or not he'd be the target of her wrath when she found out.

Turned out, he didn't need to worry about how her brother would react because when he rounded the corner to head back to their table, there was someone sitting in his seat.

Xavier Gray.

He was animatedly talking to Josie when Callan walked up. "We need to reshoot the scene from this morning about—"

"Excuse me," Callan interrupted. "I believe you're in my spot."

Xavier's gaze panned up, taking all of Callan in. He could see the thoughts ticking away in Xavier's mind as he began to put two and two together. "Wait . . . what?"

The cameras around them moved ever so slightly closer, and Callan wondered if they had known Xavier was coming. Had they set this up?

"Uh, we were having dinner," Josie spoke up, motioning to Callan. "That *is* actually Callan's seat."

"Callan?" Xavier sounded incredulous. "You mean Cal Walsh? My opponent? Are you trying to leave me and be his assistant or something?"

Josie shook her head. "No, we're just friends grabbing dinner together."

Xavier stood and sized up Callan, getting a lot closer to him than was necessary. Callan was significantly taller than Xavier, so he towered over him, but that didn't stop Xavier from sidling up to him anyway.

"Is this a . . . a date?" Xavier asked, motioning between Josie and Callan. "Are you two out on a date right now?"

Josie's face darkened, blush creeping up her cheeks.

"We are," Callan confirmed, speaking for the both of them. "A date I'd like to get back to, if you don't mind."

Xavier moved away from the table, but a vein in his neck was pulsing, and Callan could see the fury building in the tension in his body. "Josie, can I speak to you for a minute?" he said through clenched teeth.

She shook her head. "We can talk tomorrow. I'm busy right now, Xav."

He squeezed his fists, his mouth set in a firm line. "Don't bother coming to work tomorrow," Xavier said. "You clearly don't give a shit about my career. You're fired."

With that, Xavier stormed away, and one of the camera crews followed after him.

"Fired?" Callan asked her. "Are you okay?"

She waved a hand like it was no big deal. "He fires me at least once a week. It's just part of the tantrum he always throws."

Callan couldn't imagine how hard that must be to work with and what a hostile environment she dealt with.

"The annoying part is that any minute now, my mother is going to call me to yell at me for upsetting him." She sighed. "He's probably calling her right now."

Sure enough, her cell phone started buzzing where it sat on the table beside her.

She silenced the call, sighing as she did so.

Leaning in closer to the table, Callan dropped his voice to a whisper. "Do you want to get out of here?"

Her eyes widened as she looked up at him and then glanced around at the cameras trained on them. "Just us?" she whispered in response.

He nodded, pulled out his wallet, and put a few bills down on the table, and then he stood and offered her his hand.

She reached around her back and unfastened the belt that

was holding the microphone. Placing it on the table, she stood and took his hand.

He removed his microphone and handed it to the camera guy. "Peace out, Boy Scout."

The cameraman looked unsure of what to do. "Should we come with you guys?"

Callan shook his head. "No. We're done filming."

Josie grinned and practically skipped out of the restaurant at his side. "Come on. I want to take you somewhere . . ."

"Where are we going?" he asked.

She winked at him before climbing into the passenger seat of his car. "You'll see."

CHAPTER FIFTEEN

"So, tell me the truth," Callan began, running his finger down her bare arm as she lay in his arms. They were completely naked and in her bed in her apartment—a place she never brought men, but for some reason, she wanted Callan there.

She rarely had a one-night stand or hooked up with guys, but when she did, it was always at their house or a hotel. She wasn't one to have people in her space, considering how invasive her life already was. But having Callan here, in her bed, was comforting and all the things she hadn't thought she wanted.

"What truth?" she asked, stifling a yawn. She was satiated and still coming down from the high of her last orgasm.

"Your brother showing up at the restaurant—was that staged?" he asked.

Josie let out an audible sigh. "Well, no one gave me a heads-up, but if I had to guess, producers sent him there to catch us on purpose. Makes for good ratings."

He nodded. That made sense. It was a dramatic moment, and he had no doubt that it would play well on camera. "Is that why you weren't worried when he fired you?"

"Yep," Josie replied. "Guarantee he knows it was a setup. He's not going to think there's anything actually happening between us. Our mother will tell him that, too."

Hell, her mother would probably tell him it was all a stunt to sidetrack Callan before the big fight. She'd absolutely refused to do so—telling her mother that was a line she wasn't going to cross—but at the same time, she wanted to spend time with Callan. So . . . what was she doing?

Was she doing exactly what her mother wanted?

She hated that idea.

"I don't know how you do it," Callan murmured, placing kisses against her temple as he pulled her tighter against his chest. "This on-air life twenty-four-seven. These scripted scenes. How do you know what's real anymore?"

Josie felt a lump growing in her throat, threatening to silence her. She'd been dwelling on this same question for years and had fewer answers now than when she'd started.

"Honestly?" she asked, lifting her chin to be at eye-level with him. "I'm not entirely sure I do."

"Before my mother passed away, she used to always do this exercise with me," Callan started explaining. "It was a gratitude type of thing, but she called it 'three truths.' The point was to live as authentically, ambitiously, and gratefully as possible because you're always striving toward your truths. She'd always ask me in the morning—what are your three truths today?"

"That's really sweet," Josie remarked. "I'm sorry about your mother. Can I ask what happened?"

"Ovarian cancer. About five years ago." He lifted his chin slightly, as if distancing himself from the words he was speaking. "I'm okay now."

She didn't respond, her heart heavy for him.

After running his hand through her curls, he traced patterns on her shoulder with his finger. "What are your three truths today, Jos?"

She thought about his question and realized it wasn't as

easy as it had seemed at first. "Well, my first truth is that I'm happy right now. Truly content just being here with you."

"Mmm." He kissed her gently on the lips and then drew back. "What else?"

"I'm ... hmm ..." She couldn't think of anything else and was going blank. "I don't know. What are your three truths?"

Callan gave her a small smile, the kind where just the very edges of his lips curled up into a near smirk. "That's easy. One—I'm nervous about the fight on Saturday. Two—I'm aching to be inside you again. And three ... well, I think I am really starting to like you."

Josie chuckled. "Gee, thanks."

"I'm serious," he continued, his face stoic and poised as he spoke. "I didn't come here looking for a relationship or looking to date, but ... well, I'd be open to it."

Warmth filled Josie's heart at his admission. "I've never ... never felt this close to anyone so quickly," she shared.

"Your second truth," he pointed out. Leaning forward, he kissed her gently. "What's your third?"

"My third truth ..." She paused for a moment, thinking about his words and what they could be. "My third truth is that I'd be open to it too."

Had she just told him she wanted a relationship with him? Excitement filled her at the very idea.

"So ..." Callan began. "We're doing the damn thing ... huh?"

She grinned, taking in the idea piece by piece. "Well ... at least until you go back to Los Angeles," she pointed out. "What would happen then?"

Callan shrugged his shoulders. "Los Angeles isn't that far. And, there are jobs out there, whereas you haven't been able to find any here."

That comment stung slightly, but she knew he wasn't wrong. She'd applied to hundreds of places and been turned down everywhere. It was like being a chef was not in the cards for her—at least not here in Vegas.

Still, there was something about the way he said it that sounded like he knew something she didn't.

"Are you asking me to move to Los Angeles with you?"

He looked sheepish, glancing down and then back up at her. "I'm just saying it's an option. We have a lot of options . . ."

So why did it feel like there was a countdown clock on them?

CHAPTER SIXTEEN

"Are you awake?" Callan whispered in Josie's ear the next morning.

"Mmm," she mumbled and then rolled into his chest to cuddle tighter with him. "Barely."

He ran a hand down her arm, loving the soft feeling of her skin against his. He didn't want to move, didn't want to pull apart. Having her in his arms like this . . . it was everything. He'd never stuck around with a woman long enough to really appreciate how nice it was just to hold her. He was always on the move, always going, but this? This was quiet and gentle and a break from the monotony of his life.

Gym. Work. Home.

That was his entire life, and frankly, he was beginning to wonder if that was as fulfilling as he'd thought. Being around Josie was intoxicating. A little taste and he wanted more. Even if he couldn't offer her much right now, he knew he didn't want to say goodbye.

"What if I told you I ordered us breakfast?" he whispered.

Her eyes popped open. "I could wake up for breakfast."

Callan laughed at the excitement on her face. It was a hell of a lot better than the sadness he'd seen after their conversation last night. "We have a little time before it arrives," he said, leaning closer to her and kissing her neck right above her collarbone.

She moaned lightly, curving her body into his. "Really . . ."

"Really," he confirmed, running his hands down her side until he reached her thigh. Slipping his hand between her legs, he dipped a finger inside her.

Josie gasped, pressing her hips into his palm. "Oh, God ..."

Soft, gentle strokes across her clit and she was soon writhing beneath him. He leaned down and flicked his tongue across her nipples, and she arched her back in response. She wanted more, and he was going to give it to her.

He drew her nipple between his lips, sucking and pushing his tongue against the tip. She wrapped her arms around his neck, pulled him closer, and rocked her hips. He pushed a second finger inside her and used his thumb to swirl circles around her clit.

"Ah!" she cried out, sinking her teeth into his shoulder as her orgasm started to flood her senses.

Removing his hand, he pushed her legs apart and settled between them. Driving his hard cock against her entrance, he filled her to the hilt just as her climax reached its peak. Her legs wrapped around his waist, pulling him tighter into her, but he thrust quickly and forcefully until he was spilling over into her.

Leaning his weight on his elbows, he stilled. She was so warm, so tight, that he could hardly see straight. Feeling her coming around his dick had set off his own orgasm so powerfully that he could hardly catch his breath.

Knock, knock, knock.

"I bet that's our breakfast," Callan said, carefully standing and looking for his pants. Finally, he found them and slid them on, grabbing a shirt off the ground next as he headed for the door. "Eggs and bacon, coming right up!"

Her apartment was small but cozy, and he found himself

admiring it as he walked through the living room and toward the front door. When he opened the front door, the delivery man handed him a bag of food and Callan handed him some bills as a tip.

Locking the door behind him, he walked over to the kitchen counter and placed the bag down. Josie was still in the bedroom and hadn't come out yet, but her phone was sitting on the counter. It buzzed, and he happened to glance down at it.

A text message from Xavier popped up on the screen.

Are you with Walsh?

The phone buzzed again, a second text appearing.

Keep him distracted as long as you can.

"What the fuck?" Callan whispered to himself, picking up the phone and glancing at the messages. He looked back toward the bedroom and then at the phone again. A nerve-racking thought entered his mind—what if this was the plan all along?

Distract him from training for the fight with a dalliance, only to ensure Gray had the advantage.

The thought was dubious, but . . . was it?

After all, she'd been the one to admit that sometimes she didn't even know what was real anymore in her life. What if this had all been fake?

"God, that smells good," Josie said, walking into the room as she pulled a sweatshirt on over her head. "I'm starving."

He placed her phone down on the counter, saying nothing.

"I have to go train."

She paused, knitting her brows as she glanced down at her phone on the counter and then up at him. There was no doubt she was trying to figure out why he'd been holding it.

"Okay?" She said it like it was a question, as if she wasn't sure why he was telling her. "Do you have to go right now?"

He nodded his head, trying to avoid eye contact with her. "Enjoy the breakfast. I'm going to head out."

"Callan, what's going on?" She perched on a stool at the counter and propped herself up on her elbows. "You're being very..."

"Distracted?" He tossed out the phrase like it was a bomb set to go off. His jaw clenched at the thought, and he tried everything to tell himself it wasn't what he was thinking.

She nodded but seemed to continue to play innocent. "I guess distracted describes it. Are you okay?"

"I just need to get to the gym." He headed back into the bedroom and grabbed his keys off the nightstand. "I'll see you later, okay?"

"Okay." She stood and walked over to him, pushing up on her toes to kiss him.

He gave her a quick peck that lacked as much authenticity as this entire situation. "Bye."

With that, he walked out the door and made the decision then and there. He was recommitting himself to training and leaving her—and whatever they'd had between them—behind.

He only made it as far as the car before he heard her shouting his name.

"Callan!" Josie called after him just as he was climbing into the driver's side of his car. "Callan! Wait!"

He paused, stepping back out of the car and facing her.

He really didn't want to have this conversation. "What is it, Josie?"

"You read my phone." She stated it like it was a fact.

Well, at least they were both on the same page now.

He didn't refute her statement, but the muscles in his jaw clenched.

"We need to talk about this," she continued. "You can't just walk out thinking whatever it is you're thinking."

"And what am I thinking, Jos?" He stepped closer, his fists squeezing into balls. For her to actually deny what he'd just seen was bullshit, and he wasn't about to let it go. "That this has all been a trick? That you've just been using me for almost a week now to distract me from why I'm really here?"

Had any of it been real? Or had he just been falling for a con?

She shook her head, a panicked look spreading across her face. "That's not true. It's not what you think . . ."

"You're the one who told me you don't even know what's real anymore," he reminded her. Anger swirled in his gut, and as much as he wanted to let this go and get in the car, he felt like he couldn't stop himself from speaking his mind. "How am I supposed to believe you now? Everything in your life is a lie."

The words rolled off his tongue before he could even realize what he was saying.

The look on her face was like he'd just slapped her. Her eyes widened, hurt swirled in her green irises. But it was gone in a flash. She set her jaw, breathing in fire as her eyes flamed with anger.

"Me? What about you?" She pointed a finger at him. "You and your team are just using me to up your fame. That's what this whole 'date' was—not just for me but for you. You don't think I know that your social media presence is lacking? That you're only hanging out with me to boost your own profile with your audience?"

"That is not fair—"

"How? You said I'm using you, but really...you're using me." She crossed her arms over her chest.

He didn't know how to refute her statement when it... wasn't wrong.

They stood silently staring at each other for a minute, and then Callan took a deep breath and released it. "It sounds like none of this has been real on cither side."

"Maybe it hasn't," she agreed, though the hurt radiating in her eyes tore at him.

Had they just been lying to each other this entire time? Was there anything real here?

"It's probably best we end things now." He looked down at his feet to avoid seeing her pain. He hadn't wanted to hurt her...to use her...and yet, he'd done exactly that. But to be fair, she'd been using him to distract herself this entire time too.

"You're probably right." She crossed her arms over her chest. "I'll see you on Saturday in the cage."

He nodded, even though the upcoming fight was the furthest thing from his mind. He opened his driver's side door and climbed into the front seat.

She didn't try to stop him. She didn't say anything. She just stood there with her arms folded over her chest as he drove away.

He knew he was doing the right thing...so why did it feel so wrong?

CHAPTER SEVENTEEN

Two days.

It had been two days since he'd seen Josie, two long days of second-guessing his every decision. Callan slammed his fist into the heavy bag and then stepped back, regrouping. The center was emptied out today—completely dedicated to him and Xavier to use for training for tomorrow's fight.

"Good. Again." Ferguson coached him from a few feet away. "You need to square your shoulders when you're striking. Focus on technique."

Callan repeated the move a few more times, listening to every bit of feedback his trainer had for him along the way. Still, there was an inauthenticity in his hits. A weakness that hadn't been there before.

"You've got to focus, Walsh," Ferguson chided, coming around to the back of the heavy bag and holding it still. "Where's your head?"

"Sorry," Callan replied, shaking his hands out and stretching his neck from side to side. "I'm going to be here. I promise."

"Promises aren't good enough. You've got less than twenty-four hours until the defining fight of your career. Are you just going to sit down and let him pummel you into the ground? Or are you going to fight your ass off and win?"

Callan clapped his fist into the palm of his opposite hand. "I'm going to fucking fight."

"Good." Ferguson smacked him on the back of his shoulders. "Put her out of your mind."

He arched a brow. "Who?"

"Whatever girl has you twisted up inside." Ferguson crossed his arms over his chest. "I recognize the signs of heartbreak, kid. You've got it written all over your face."

Ferguson was at least twice his age and a grandfather to two young girls. Callan had no doubt that his trainer was wise enough to sense the emotional disturbance he'd been experiencing for the last two days.

"It's that obvious, huh?"

His trainer nodded. "But you need to get your head out of your ass and back into the game. You've got one shot at this."

They finished up their session together, and Ferguson instructed him to take the rest of the day off for resting. He was supposed to ice his joints and get a massage. Anything and everything that would ease his mind and ready his body for tomorrow.

"And get laid while you're at it," Ferguson said. "Get out that frustration. Or better yet, store it all up and take it out on Gray in the ring."

If only that was the Gray he wanted to take his sexual frustrations out on.

Callan headed back to the hotel, arriving in his penthouse not long after. He collapsed on the bed with a loud sigh but moved slightly when he felt something small and sharp sticking in his back. Reaching around for it, he pulled out an earring that had been buried in his sheets. It was a small gold hoop, and he immediately recognized it as Josie's from one of their last nights together.

Placing it on the bedside table, he stared at it. He tried to think of what it was about Josie that intrigued him so much. Why he couldn't get her out of his brain.

Their time together had been so short. It didn't make sense that he was this invested in her already . . . and yet he was. He'd thought of her every morning when waking up, and she was the last thing he thought about every night before falling asleep. Hell, she was all he thought about all day long.

Meeting her and being with her this last week . . . it had felt like he'd found a piece of himself that had long since been missing. And now it was gone, and so was she.

He felt empty.

The things that used to drive him—his career, the next fight, ambition—didn't hold as much regard for him anymore. Instead, all he could think about was what life would be like if he settled down . . . found a wife . . . got married and had kids.

Josie made him think of those things. He never had before meeting her.

But it was like a switch had flipped in his brain.

Carefully, he fingered the earring on his bedside table and held it up to the light. He could almost see her reflection in its edges. Pulling out his phone, he debated whether or not to call her. He could invite her over for the afternoon, get a couple's massage, spend the evening having crazy, hot sex . . .

But he couldn't seem to press the button on his phone. Instead, he just put it back down and buried his head in the pillows.

Tomorrow was coming way too soon.

CHAPTER EIGHTEEN

"Why you looking so down, Jos?" Marcus, her baby brother, asked as she stared out the window of Xavier's penthouse.

She turned to face him, trying to wipe any signs of emotion away. "I'm not. I'm just tired. I haven't been sleeping well."

Marcus stood and crossed the room, taking the seat next to her. He put his hand on her shoulder and looked her squarely in the eyes. "Bullshit."

"What?" She fumbled for words, trying to figure out how to respond. Marcus always knew when she was feeling down, and now was no exception.

"I heard about the network wanting you to branch out into your own show," he said. "I heard about the date with Callan and Xav's reaction. Hell, the whole world heard about his reaction."

She swallowed hard, not wanting to think about Callan. Unfortunately, that was impossible these days with the fight coming up tomorrow.

"You've been moping around the last two days like someone killed your cat," Marcus pointed out. "Something is obviously up."

Jos looked out at the strip, which she could see from the window of the hotel they were staying at. "It might not have just been the one date," she admitted for the first time.

Marcus's brows lifted in surprise, then he nodded slowly.

"So, it wasn't a stunt for the show? It was real?"

She really didn't know the answer to that question anymore, but it had been as real for her as she knew how to be. That might not be saying a lot, but it had meant a lot to her.

Josie just nodded to confirm.

Marcus let out a low whistle. "Falling for your brother's opponent. Jos, that's a big one."

"I know...but it's over," she assured him. "It was over before it even started."

"Why?" Marcus frowned. "If you really liked him, I'm sure Xav would have come around eventually."

Again, she didn't have an answer. There was no logical reason why they'd split up, but their fight had been big enough that breaking up was exactly what happened. Tears pricked in the corners of her eyes as she swallowed hard, trying to push away the emotion. Unsuccessful at her attempts to hold them back, one of her tears slid down her cheek.

"Aw, Jos." Marcus reached forward and gave her a hug. "You're really broken up over this guy?"

She couldn't speak out loud without sobbing, so she said nothing. But her answer was loud and clear.

Leaving Callan had been a mistake...but one she didn't know how to fix. He thought she was using him to help Xavier win the fight...and he wasn't wrong. Josie's mother had wanted exactly that. Josie had never agreed to it and had been vehemently opposed to it, actually, but that didn't mean the plan didn't exist.

And she'd known about it.

"Marcus! Josie!" Xavier burst into the living room with a bang, letting the doors slam against the wall as he swung them open. "Are we ready?"

"For what?" Marcus asked.

"To go out. We need to celebrate for tomorrow," Xavier said, already pouring himself a glass of Scotch at the bar cart in the hotel room. "We're trained. We're ready. We're going to kick ass. Let's do a little good-luck outing."

Josie shook her head. "Definitely not. You need to be in bed early and getting all the rest you can for tomorrow."

"Fuck that shit. I'm going out." Xavier downed his glass and returned to the bar cart for another. "We'll be fine."

"Xav, I'm serious. What would your trainer say? He told you to rest tonight."

Xavier waved his hand as if to say he couldn't care less. "What he doesn't know won't hurt him."

Josie sighed, frustrated with her brother. She knew there was nothing she could really say to change his mind. Once he'd decided that this was what he was doing, the man was a bulldozer at full steam.

"Fine, but one drink and that's it," Josie tried for a compromise.

Xavier rolled his eyes at her, a smirk on the corner of his lips. "Sure thing, *Mom*."

It wasn't like she liked being a buzzkill, but it was her job as his assistant to keep him in line. A fucking hard job at that.

"Come on. The driver will take us down to the Bellagio," Xavier said a few minutes later, looking up from his phone. "He's outside."

Josie nodded, not really looking forward to the night out. She was definitely going to be a babysitter.

Sure enough, when they arrived at the Bellagio, they went straight to an exclusive club off the top floor with a balcony that overlooked the strip that few people even had access to, and Xavier started pounding shots.

"Don't you think you should slow down?" she asked him after his third shot, putting her hand on his arm. "You've got the fight tomorrow."

"Not until tomorrow night," he reminded her. "I've got all day to sober up. And I can still beat his ass with a drink in one hand."

Xavier's words came out slow and with a slight slur to them. He was definitely already intoxicated and on his way to black-out drunk if he kept going.

The cameraman and producer from their reality show chose that moment to show up.

"Hey, we want to film his last night before the fight," the producer told Josie. "Do you want to do an ITM?"

ITMs were in-the-moments, where she spoke directly to the camera behind the scenes about what she was feeling at the time they were filming.

"Sure," she agreed. Hell, anything to get her away from Xavier.

"Let's set up over there." The cameraman pointed to a small alcove that offered them some privacy. She waited while they set up the equipment needed and put a chair against the wall for her to sit in.

She sat and fluffed her hair out, getting herself ready.

These ITMs were a part of being a reality television star, but damn...she hated them. The producers always threw her curveball questions, trying to get her off her game or to say something salacious for the show. It was a battle to stay grounded and keep her head straight during shooting.

"How do you feel about Xavier's chances in the fight tomorrow?" the producer asked her, sitting across from her but out of the way of the camera's view.

"I feel like Xavier's going to have a hard time in the fight tomorrow," Josie admitted, making sure to repeat part of the question in her response. It was another part of filming ITMs— always repeating the question so that they could play the clip without the producer's voice asking the question.

"Why do you think that?" the producer asked.

"I think he will have a hard time tomorrow because he is out getting drunk the night before," she explained. "It isn't exactly a recipe for success."

The producer nodded. "Do you think your brother has a drinking problem?"

Josie paused, trying to decide how honest to be and what should or shouldn't be on camera. "No," she finally said. "My brother doesn't have a drinking problem. He does, however, have a maturity problem."

She wasn't sure that was entirely true, but that was all she was willing to divulge on camera. To be honest, it had been a while since she'd seen Xavier without a drink in his hand.

"Switching gears," the producer said, looking down at a clipboard in her hands. "Let's talk about romance."

"Romance?" she questioned, not sure what she was referring to.

"Tell me about your date with Callan Walsh."

Josie's chin lifted slightly, caution overtaking her. She didn't want to talk about it on camera. She didn't want to share this part of herself with the world. It was private … It was *hers*.

And it was over.

An ache settled in her chest.

"Um … my date with Callan Walsh was lovely," she finally said, keeping things as vague as she could. "He was a perfect gentleman."

"Are you going to go out with him again?"

Josie shook her head quickly. "I have no plans to go out with him again."

"Why not?" the producer dug a little further.

She shrugged, not really knowing how to answer that question. "We're just two different people."

The producer looked disappointed but asked her a few more questions about Callan and her brother and the upcoming fight. Josie answered them all as vaguely as she could, staying safe and . . . boring.

She didn't give them any exciting sound bites, and they knew it. Sure, she was going to hear from Jamie Sessions about it. He would probably call her and complain, encourage her to open up more. But she didn't care. She honestly didn't care about the show anymore at all.

The thought struck her hard.

I don't care about the show.

This show—which had been her life for the last five years—felt insignificant now. It didn't feel like her or who she had grown into.

When had that happened? When had she become someone else?

She couldn't help but wonder if Callan had anything to do with that. Meeting him, falling for him, the conversations they had late into the night . . . it had pushed her to think harder about what she wanted in life. It had awoken a feeling of . . . dissatisfaction in her.

Not with him but with her current situation.

He'd shown her what life could be like, and she wanted more. She wanted that connection, that closeness of having a partner by her side. Someone who would do anything for her, no matter how crazy or out there.

They'd literally buried a body together in the desert.

She smiled slightly, the corners of her lips twitching up. She hadn't thought about their late-night tryst in a few days, but it still amused her. His openness to following along on her crazy schemes . . . was special. *He* was special.

And in doing that, she was realizing just how *un*-special her life really was.

Despite being a famous reality television star that other people considered privileged and lucky and special and all those things they wished they could be . . . the truth was, she was miserable.

That was a hard fact to accept, but it was true.

She sat in front of the camera answering questions, all the while thinking about who she really was and what she wanted to be.

Crash!

A loud clanging noise disturbed the interview, and the camera swiveled around in the direction of where Xavier was sitting. Or . . . where he had been sitting.

Now he was on the floor, a spilled drink all over him.

"Xav!" Josie stood up and ran over to him. "Are you okay?"

"Fi-Fi-Fine," he stuttered out, a slur on his lips. "I'm great, Josie girl. How's you?"

The cameraman and producer stood back and just watched the scene unfolding.

"Can you help me get him up?" she called out to the cameraman, who was a giant of a man and could have easily helped her lift her brother up.

The cameraman ignored her and just moved closer, zooming the camera in on Xavier's face.

"Seriously? You're not going to help?" Josie threw her hands up and tried to push Xavier into a seated position herself, but he was too big for her.

"Jos!" Marcus came around the corner, having been in the bathroom when everything happened. "What happened?"

Her brother helped her lift Xavier back onto the chair, but Xavier's head dangled against his chest. He was completely passed out.

"He drank too much," Josie said, pointing out the obvious. "Can you call security up here?"

Marcus pulled out his phone and dialed security's number. Moments later, they arrived and hooked an arm around both sides of Xavier. Josie watched as they carried him back toward the hotel. Luckily, they had booked a room in advance just in case they needed to crash here. It looked like that was exactly what Xavier would be doing.

Josie, on the other hand, was going home.

The cameraman followed Xavier out, recording every moment of his embarrassing stunt and doing absolutely nothing to help.

It pissed her the fuck off.

Heading home, Josie couldn't help but think about what she was doing with her life. Why was she in this show that didn't give a shit about her? If that was her falling down drunk, they'd rather film it than prevent it from happening in the first place.

She wasn't safe with them. She wasn't safe in her own home.

Swallowing hard, she realized what she needed to do as she crawled into her bed about thirty minutes later.

Now she just needed the courage to actually do it.

CHAPTER NINETEEN

"Are you fucking ready?"

Callan slammed his fist against his other palm.

Ferguson placed both his hands on Callan's shoulders. "I said . . . are you *fucking* ready?"

"I'm ready!" Callan responded, nearly yelling as they stood in the back room waiting to be called out onto the main stage where the cage was set up and ready for tonight's fight.

"Get pumped!" Ferguson clapped him on the shoulders and made a grunting noise. "We're going to beat his ass. We're going to win!"

"Yes!" Callan shouted.

A knock came from the doorway, and they both turned to face it. Expecting to see a show runner telling him it was time to come out, Callan was surprised when he saw Josie standing there instead.

"Hi . . ." Her voice was soft, timid almost.

"Jos," he began, taking a step closer to her.

Ferguson glanced between the two of them, clearly putting the pieces together. "Uh, I'm going to go grab a water. I'll be back in a minute."

Callan nodded, grateful that his trainer, and friend, was able to pick up on his need for privacy. He left them alone, and Josie walked farther into the room.

"I just wanted to say good luck tonight." She pulled her bag up higher on her shoulder.

"Thanks." He realized then that she had a suitcase with her and a large bag over her shoulder. "Are you going somewhere?"

She glanced down at her suitcase and then back up at him. "Just taking a trip."

There was something behind what she was saying, and he wondered what she really was doing.

"Jos." He stepped closer, trying hard to focus on the moment and not the fact that her beautiful face looked like he should be kissing a line across her jaw or the fact that the tiny pink dress she was wearing was the perfect contrast against her dark skin. He wanted to pull her into his arms and kiss her, make her his again . . . but that option was off the table.

Hell, he'd chosen that.

She had just been distracting him to try to help her brother win this fight. He had to keep reminding himself of that.

So . . . why was she here wishing him luck? Why was she leaving?

"Where are you going, Jos?" he asked again, digging for the truth he could tell she didn't want to give him.

She lifted her chin slightly, a mist filling in under her eyes. "New York."

"What?" He balked. "For how long?"

"I'm moving there," she admitted, not looking him straight in the eyes now. She was avoiding his gaze, looking down at her feet instead. There was more she wasn't telling him, and he needed to know.

"Jos . . . talk to me." He grabbed the strap of the bag on her shoulder and pulled it off, placing it on the ground. Then he took her hand and pulled her closer to him. "Talk to me. Why are you leaving?"

"I called in some favors and got an interview for the

Institute of Culinary Education," she explained. "I'm going to try to go back to school. Make my way as a chef in New York City."

He paused, not sure how to respond to her. He was proud of her. He wanted the best for her, and pursuing cooking... that was everything she had wanted. Plus, he'd heard from Rockport that that was one of the best schools in the world for culinary arts. If she could go there... Hell, he'd champion it.

But she'd also be going to the other side of the country. Whatever was between them would really be over.

"I... I think that's amazing, Jos. You deserve that. You deserve to pursue your cooking," he finally said, running his hands up and down her arms. "When are you leaving?"

"Now. My flight is in two hours."

He swallowed hard. "So you're not staying for the fight?"

She shook her head.

"And the show?" he asked, wondering what she was going to do about her spot in the reality television world.

"I quit," she admitted, chewing the corner of her lip. A slight chuckle left her lips. "I even shut down my Instagram page."

He raised his brows. "Seriously?"

The woman he'd accused of just using him for fame and trying to sabotage his fight was... giving it all up? He was beginning to think he might have been wrong from the start. Guilt settled into his stomach and began burrowing its way to his heart.

She nodded, a slight tremble in her chin when she looked at him. "It's over."

He suddenly wanted to hold her, the urge to wrap his arms around her and never let go was fighting at his will. "Maybe...

maybe I'll come to New York City and visit you?"

Josie adamantly shook her head. "Don't."

"Why?" he asked, confused at her sudden admission.

"You need to be here and in Los Angeles. You need to be who you are." Josie glanced down at her fidgeting hands. "And I . . . I need to be who I am. And those are just two different people."

"Jos . . ." he began, reaching for her hand. "I meant what I said when I told you I wanted to give this a shot. I still do."

He couldn't help but pour the truth out. Now that he knew she had given up everything he'd thought was pulling her away from him, how could he not? Hell, it felt like she'd done this for them . . . to give them a real chance. But from the way she spoke, it sounded like she was doing this for herself . . . without him.

And that broke his heart.

"I know you did," she replied. "I know you meant every word, and I did too . . . then. But now?" She paused for a moment, as if carefully considering her words. "We aren't good for each other, Callan."

"How can you say that?" he countered, even though he knew exactly what she meant. Every day he'd spent curled in bed with her was a day he'd neglected training for today's fight. Every night he'd not been able to sleep because he'd been thinking about her, worrying about her . . . it could cost him this fight. If he did win tonight, it would be by a slim margin, and he only had himself to blame for that.

"You know it's true," she told him. "I . . . I have to go."

"Okay." He didn't know what else to say, but he felt like he should apologize. Hell, he needed to apologize. "Jos . . . I'm sorry."

"You didn't do anything wrong," she responded. "I'm the one who should be sorry. My show ... my life ... it's a mess. I didn't mean to involve you in that."

He wanted to reply and tell her everything was fine, that she should stay here ... with him. That she should move to Los Angeles and start over there. He wanted to tell her that he realized he was wrong and that she wasn't all about fame and fortune. That he understood now.

But he said nothing. Instead, he just nodded.

"Bye, Callan," she said softly, squeezing his hand. "Get in that cage and show everyone who you are—who I know you can be."

"Thank you." He squeezed her hand back in response. "Fly safe."

With that, she turned and walked out of the room. He stood there staring at the doorway.

"Safe to return?" Ferguson asked, poking his head around the corner.

Callan nodded, motioning for his trainer to come in. "Yeah."

"You good?" he asked, clapping a hand on Callan's shoulder. "You need to talk?"

That was the last thing he wanted to do. Hell, all he really wanted to do right now was get out in the ring and fight. He was so far from good. So far from okay. He didn't even know what he was feeling or how to describe it.

All he knew was he'd made a mistake. He'd let the woman he could have spent forever with slip between his fingers.

She was gone.

It was too late now. He didn't have time to mourn the loss, dwell on the things he couldn't change. No, he had a fight to win. He had to put his best foot forward, or all of this would be for nothing. She was leaving to be a chef. He was here in the cage. Their lives were going in different directions, and that was just the way it was.

He had to accept it.

"Let's do this," Callan responded, powdering his hands and pulling on gloves.

Ferguson opened a fresh bottle of water and poured some into Callan's mouth. Callan took the drink and swallowed.

A show runner came moments later, calling them to the cage. Ferguson put a cape on Callan—which Callan always found a little ridiculous, but it came with the territory. Next, he put on his last fight's belt, a giant, gaudy, gold contraption that wrapped around his waist.

He'd never particularly liked the showman part of being a fighter in the cage, but he understood that the fans loved it. After all, they were the reason he had a job to begin with. There was something so inspiring about having people look up to him, wanting the best from him and considering him their hero.

It was intoxicating.

As Callan thought about it, he realized he could understand why Josie had gotten so wrapped up in the reality television world. It was hard to let go of being a public figure when so many people looked up to him and relied on him. It was a power trip, but it was also . . . an identity.

Callan had no idea who he'd be if he wasn't a fighter. This was him. This was his identity.

He wondered now who Josie was . . . or who she would be. She'd just shed everything in her life that had made up who she was. Would she change? Would she be someone he didn't even recognize? As silly as it might seem, the fact that she'd closed her Instagram alone was mind boggling to him. As insignificant as it sounded, that was a huge part of her job as a reality television star. They'd never been together for more than a few hours without her posting to her Instagram feed.

Part of him was even sad that he wouldn't be able to secretly check up on her while she was in New York. He'd have no way of following her or knowing what she was doing. Not that he planned to stalk her or anything.

He'd just miss her.

Hell, he missed her already, and she wasn't even gone yet.

Had they made a mistake?

"Cal, get your head in the game," Ferguson said, trying to snap him out of his thoughts. "Where the fuck did you go?"

Callan looked up at his trainer. "What?"

"I've been talking to you for the last few minutes, and you're just zoned out."

"Sorry," Callan responded, adjusting the belt around his waist. "I'm just gearing up for the fight. We ready?"

The show runner looked at both of them and motioned for them to follow him. "We're just waiting on you," he said. "The crowd is hyped and ready to go."

Callan nodded. "Let's do it."

They walked through the center's back hallways and came to the entrance for the main arena. Callan could hear the crowd already roaring from the other side of the double doors. Lights flashed through the windowpanes on the doors, and he started to feel excitement building in his gut.

This was what he'd prepared for over the last year. This was who he was.

Putting his head down, he charged through the double

doors just as the announcer called him out. The cage stood tall in the middle of the arena, bleachers all around completely packed with people. They were cheering so loudly that he couldn't even make out what anyone was saying. It was just a roar that coursed through his veins and increased his excitement tenfold with every step he took toward the cage.

When he finally reached the entrance, he spotted his opponent on the other side. Xavier had been called out before him and was already pandering to the crowd. He spotted a few members of the Gray family around the sidelines, but there was one family member noticeably missing.

He tried to push thoughts of Josie out of his mind.

Now wasn't the time.

"You got this," Ferguson shouted in Callan's ear, and he was barely able to hear him over the crowd. "Get in there."

Callan nodded and headed into the cage with his head slightly bent down, deliberately projecting a menacing look on his face. He clenched his jaw, flared his nose, and charged right up to the referee. The ref held his gloved hand up in the air as the announcer introduced him to the crowd.

The crowd went wild. People were stomping on the bleacher stands and pumping their fists in the air. It was all the encouragement he needed. A fire lit in him that he'd never felt before.

It was time to kick ass.

CHAPTER TWENTY

Xavier Gray's fist landed on Callan's shoulder, knocking him back a few steps. Pain split through Callan's arm and ricocheted around his body, but it didn't last long. He rallied quickly and dodged the next blow with a sidestep and then sent a jab directly into Gray's side. Gray returned his jab immediately.

The bell rang, and they pulled apart and walked to opposite sides of the cage. The announcer filled the crowd in on the fight stats.

Callan went to the corner where Ferguson was standing on a platform that made him tall enough to rest his elbows on top of the cage.

"You're doing great," his trainer congratulated him. "Need some water?"

Callan nodded, pulling his mouth guard out as Ferguson squirted water into his mouth. He swallowed, refreshed by the cool drink. He was ready to get back out there. The fight had barely just started, but these things went by in a flash when he was the one in the cage.

The ref called both fighters back into the center of the cage. The bell rang, and Gray started circling around him. Callan kept his hands up, covering his face and making small jabs in Gray's direction.

Gray's leg shot out, trying to land a kick against Callan's stomach, but he dodged out of the way.

They circled again, both fighters bouncing on the balls of their feet as they approached one another.

Callan lunged forward and swung an arm around Gray's neck, pulling him into his chest as he landed repeated punches against Gray's stomach. He got at least five in before Gray twisted out and slipped away.

Again circling, they landed kicks and punches against one another. Callan landed a fist on the side of Gray's head, and a trickle of blood dripped down from Gray's brow.

Gray growled, wiping it away. He was seething as he came at Callan. Gray twisted his body around and landed a kick to the side of Callan's face.

Callan staggered backward, his vision going black for a moment as the pain seared through his jaw. He stumbled, threatening to fall over, and Gray took that as his opportunity to come in hot and heavy. With fists going a million miles an hour, Gray swiped him on either side of his face.

Putting his fists up, Callan tried to block the blows, sidestepping and bouncing backward in an attempt to get away from his attacker. Finally, he broke free of Gray's hold and got to the other side of the ring. He tasted copper and wiped at his lip, blood coming off on his gloved hand.

Callan wasn't deterred. A little blood wasn't going to stop him from winning this fight.

They circled each other again, both making jabs even though none landed. They dodged and ducked and moved around until finally the crowd began roaring for action. Going in at each other, Gray pushed his forearm against Callan's throat, shoving him backward against the cage wall. Callan's back hit the cage, and he struggled to free himself as Gray used his free hand to land punches across Callan's abs.

Sore from every blow, he twisted to the side and managed to get out of Gray's lock hold. Gray hadn't turned around yet, and Callan took that opportunity to land a kick to the back of Gray's head. Gray slammed forward into the cage wall and slumped down to the mat.

Callan pumped his arms up in the air, pandering to the crowd for his success.

The ref rushed over to Gray, checked on him, and began counting.

But Gray wasn't ready to give up. He pushed back up to his feet and cracked his neck from side to side, leveling his fists at Callan.

Gray roared, saying something Callan couldn't understand because of the mouth guard. Gray launched himself at Callan, fists flying in every direction. Caught by a right hook to the jaw, Callan fell backward again, and this time Gray climbed on top of him and shoved him into the mat. Blood went everywhere as Callan struggled to right himself. He could barely see through the blood pouring down his face, but he managed to kick up into Gray's stomach and knock him off.

Flipping back onto his feet, Callan swiped his leg against Gray's knee, taking him down to the mat. He returned Gray's earlier favor and got on top of him, this time hooking his legs up around Callan's shoulders, immobilizing his opponent.

Just as he got in a few hard swings and Gray's brow split open, the bell rang.

The ref pulled him off Gray, and he returned to his corner. The ref had to help Gray up, and he was able to make his way back to his corner.

Ferguson greeted Callan the moment he returned. "You doing okay?"

His trainer put an ice pack against his head, wiping at the blood on his face. Callan nodded and pulled out the mouth guard, parting his lips for more water. Ferguson poured some in his mouth and then squirted some over the top of his head. The cool liquid streamed down his face as Ferguson handed him a towel to wipe off.

The towel came back wet and bloody after he'd finished using it.

"You've got him," Ferguson continued. "He's down and out. Look how tired he is. You've got this."

Callan nodded, putting his mouth guard back in and tightening up his gloves. He was exhausted and sore all over, but there was no doubt in his mind that he could do this.

The bell rang, and the ref called them to the middle of the cage. Callan and Gray immediately started circling each other, and this time, their jabs landed. Callan felt a jab to his side every few seconds, but at the same time, his punches were landing against Gray as well.

They slammed against the cage wall, and Callan pinned his opponent there, reveling in the moment of having the upper hand. His knee slammed against Gray several times in conjunction with punches to the side of Gray's head.

Gray slumped in Callan's arms, sliding to the ground. Callan didn't let up, continuing to punch until a ref pulled him off his fallen opponent.

"Stand back! Stand back!" the ref shouted, shoving him away from Gray.

Callan stumbled backward and then righted himself. He lifted his arms in the air, roaring at the top of his lungs. The crowd was on their feet, chanting and stomping.

"Walsh! Walsh! Walsh!" the crowd screamed for his

victory, and sure enough, the announcer then called the match and declared Callan the winner.

Medics swarmed the cage and came to Gray's side, immediately helping him up and tending to his wounds. Some smelling salts were run under Gray's nose, and as he groggily came to, Callan was relieved to see him awake. As much as he was a fighter at his core, he never wanted to actually kill anyone. It was always a risk but also his worst nightmare.

A medic came to Callan next and started wiping blood off his face. Bandages were placed on his cheek, which had split open from a punch from Gray. Everything whirled around him so quickly, Callan could barely keep up with what was happening. He just went where people pushed him.

Before he knew it, Ferguson was at his side, removing his mouth guard and giving him more water. "Fucking fantastic! You did it!"

The announcer continued reading out the stats about the fight, and replays of the knockout played on big screens around the arena. A ref pulled Callan to the center of the cage as someone wrapped a giant belt around his waist.

The championship belt.

It hit Callan right then and there—he'd won. He'd won the championship. He'd won the fight for which he'd been training for the last year. Everything he'd ever wanted was right here in front of him.

So why did it feel so empty?

He couldn't help but look over toward Gray's camp and wish Josie had been there to see him win. He knew she was probably already at the airport by now, but . . . it felt lackluster without her there. What had he been doing all of this for?

This was his moment, and yet once it arrived, all he wanted

to do was share it with a woman who was on her way across the country. Sadness curled in his stomach as he thought of her, but he pushed it aside and smiled at the crowd.

This was his win, and he was going to celebrate it.

Damn his heart for saying otherwise.

CHAPTER TWENTY-ONE

One year later...

Josie looked in the mirror and took a deep breath. Her skin glowed with the highlight she'd just applied to her cheekbones and the gold shimmer around her eyes. It was the exact look she was going for, and admittedly, she felt rather pretty.

It wasn't that she didn't normally feel pretty, but it was difficult living in her skin at times. She wasn't the smallest woman out there and had the kind of curves that men killed for but women looked down on. It was a constant struggle to find parts of herself that she liked, and she completely blamed her former life on television and social media for her insecurity. Once upon a time, she'd been constantly judged on her appearance and how she looked. But now? People rarely paid attention to her anymore.

With her social media presence at zero and her focus having been on school for the last year, she had disappeared from the public eye entirely. Occasionally, a reporter would pop in here and there to see how she was doing and if there was any new information they could scoop from her. Each time, they came up empty. Her life just wasn't the exciting roller coaster ride it had been before, and she was grateful for that. With that previous excitement had come stress and drama, none of which she needed or wanted anymore.

Turning around, she glanced back over her shoulder into

the mirror and judged her dark-yellow dress. It had always been one of her favorite colors, offsetting her dark-brown skin tone perfectly. This was everything she had wanted for her graduation day.

Except for one major thing... Her family.

They'd disowned her since she'd quit the show and left Las Vegas. She'd been called a traitor to the family, as she almost cost them the entire show. The network hadn't wanted to continue filming without her. Somehow, though, they'd managed to convince them otherwise when Xavier had started dating the adult daughter of a Real Housewife. The family's publicity had skyrocketed once more, and the network decided not to pull the plug.

Josie, however, was completely left on the outskirts. Her family didn't call. They didn't write. They had never visited her in New York. It was heartbreaking, to say the least.

She thought back to a little over a year ago at this time. How different her life had been. Thoughts of Callan Walsh couldn't help but drift across her mind. They'd only spent two weeks together, but it had felt like a lifetime. She hadn't heard from him since her move to New York, but she hadn't expected to. She'd been pretty clear with him that she didn't want him to contact her or visit her.

And she appreciated that he'd respected that request.

But at the same time... her heart ached when she replayed the last time she saw him. Refusing him had been one of the most difficult things she'd ever done, and she didn't know how to bring her heart back from that.

She'd spent the last year so focused on school that she hadn't even done much socializing. Sure, she'd made a few friends with her classmates, and they occasionally grabbed a quick drink at happy hour or something like that, but dating? That was entirely off the table. The last person she'd been with was Callan, and she had no plans of moving on to anyone else anytime soon.

A knock on her door brought her back into the real world. She turned around and headed across her small one-bedroom loft to the front door. Opening it, she stopped in her tracks.

"Mom?"

Shondra Gray was standing in her building's apartment hallway, staring back at her. She was dressed to the nines in a gorgeous emerald-green pantsuit that looked absolutely elegant on her. "Hi, Josie."

"What . . . what are you doing here?" she asked, stumbling over her words with the shock of seeing her mother. *What the hell is happening? Why is Mom here? How did she even find me?*

"Hey, sister," Marcus greeted her, stepping into view beside their mother. "We're all here."

Josie stuck her head out into the hallway, and sure enough, Xavier was standing there too. He had his arm around the shoulders of a petite Asian woman who was the perfect height for his short stature. She immediately recognized the woman from the tabloids as the *Real Housewives* daughter who Xavier had been dating for the last year.

"Are you going to invite us in?" her mother asked, a small, timid smile spreading across her lips.

Josie moved to the side and made enough room for her mother and brothers to walk by her.

Shondra entered the small apartment, looking around. "This is . . . cozy."

"Mom," Marcus warned.

"It's okay. I know it's small," Josie said, not at all

embarrassed by its size. Sure, in Las Vegas she'd had a larger apartment paid for by her lucrative job, but since moving to New York City, not only was real estate smaller, but so was her budget. She'd spent most of her savings on tuition and rent for the last year, squeezing every dime she had to the point where now she needed a job ... badly.

But she wasn't stressing about it. She'd put out applications at some of the top restaurants and chains around the country. She was just waiting for one of them to bite.

"It's not that small for New York," Marcus assured her, always trying to be the family peacemaker.

"Thanks," she said, and there was an awkward moment as everyone hugged and said hello to each other. Xavier introduced his girlfriend as Jasmine Xi, and Josie was pleasantly surprised to not smell any alcohol on his breath when he hugged her.

Maybe things had changed with this new romance ...

"So ... not that it's not great to see you guys," Josie began, "but ... what are you doing here?"

Shondra spoke up first. "We're here to go to your graduation, of course."

"I ... I didn't tell you I was graduating," Josie said. "How did you know?"

"Darling, you may have stopped talking to us, but we haven't forgotten about you. I've been following everything you're doing out here, and ..." Her mother paused for a moment and then let out a long breath. "Well, I'm really proud of you. You've done amazing on your own and in your classes."

Josie put her hand to her chest, trying to calm the thumping sound of her heart as the pressure began to build and tears pricked at the corners of her eyes. "You're what?"

"I said I'm proud of you. And, if you'll have us, we'd love to be there at your graduation to celebrate your accomplishment." Shondra offered her a small smile that looked almost nervous, as if she was worried Josie was going to turn her down and say no.

"Yeah, sis," Marcus chimed in. "We'd love to come."

"Been looking forward to it all trip," Xavier echoed.

She was touched, not just at the effort they'd made to come all the way out here but at the forgiveness that was underlying everything they were saying. Her mother was letting go of the fact that she'd left the show and nearly cost them their livelihood. Her brother was forgiving the fact that she'd missed his championship fight and slept with his opponent. Sure, it was unspoken, but it was there. She hadn't even realized how much guilt she'd been holding on to until that moment. It felt like a weight had been lifted off her shoulders, and she wanted nothing more than to run into her mother's arms for a hug.

"I'd love you all to come," she said, reaching her arms out.

Shondra embraced her. "Wonderful."

Josie tried to keep the tears from running down her cheeks, but she was unsuccessful. "Thank you, guys. Thank you for supporting me. This really does mean the world to me."

"Hey," Xavier said, putting his hand on her shoulder. "We're family first."

"Xavier has something he wants to tell you," Shondra said, nudging her son.

Xav's face suddenly looked nervous, and he swallowed hard. "Yeah ... uh ... I owe you an apology."

"You? I owe you an apology for missing your fight and ... that whole thing with—"

"Walsh," Xavier finished for her. "Yeah, I know. But ...

that's not it. I, uh, well, I might have made it difficult for you to find a cooking job back in Las Vegas."

Josie scrunched her brow. "What do you mean?"

"I kind of told the entire strip that if they tried to steal you from me, I'd make sure their restaurant went under." Xavier rubbed a hand across the back of his neck, looking sheepish. "Not that I even really have that kind of power, but you know . . . fame speaks for you."

"You blacklisted me?" Josie balked. "Are you fucking kidding me?"

"I know! I'm sorry," he repeated, holding his hands up in a defensive position. "I really am sorry, Jos. You were just such a great assistant to me. I thought I couldn't do it without you. I seriously thought you were the key to my success, but I've realized . . . well, I've realized I need to shape up and rely on myself. Jasmine here made me see that."

He smiled down at the woman he was with. A look of true love passed over both of their faces, and Josie felt an ache in her chest at what—or who—she was missing.

"I've stopped drinking. Sober nine months now," he continued. "I also started a Big Brother-type program for kids in Vegas and the surrounding area who need to get off the street and get into the gym. Help channel that aggression in healthier ways. It's doing really well, and we're helping a lot of teens."

Josie was still angry from his admission, but she had to admit . . . he really did seem like a changed man. There was just something about his spirit, about his attitude, that came off as an entirely different person. He didn't seem like her angry, hotheaded brother for whom she'd spent the last five years working. No, he seemed calm. Content, almost. He seemed . . . happy.

She was glad for him, even if she was still fucking pissed about what he had done.

"That's impressive, Xav," Josie said. "But are you telling me I can't work in Las Vegas ever again now?"

He shook his head. "Definitely not. I've righted my wrongs, and I've made sure every restaurant on the strip knows that they should hire you because you're the best damn chef they'll ever find. In fact ... I set up an interview for you, if you're interested."

Now she was just confused. "*You* got me an interview?"

He grinned like he'd just delivered the best news of his life. "Yep. Monday at noon in Vegas with Michael Rockport."

Her eyes nearly bulged out of her head. "Are you *freaking kidding* me?"

Xavier shook his head again, his grin widening. "Nope. I know how much you love that dude's show and all that crap."

Her fandom for Rockport had not lessened one iota in the last year. She still watched his cooking show daily and had dreamed of working in one of his kitchens one day. This was literally a dream come true. Any anger she previously had regarding her brother's devious plot to keep her unemployed was quickly dissipating at the news.

He sure knew how to make it up to her.

"Come on," Shondra said. "We don't have time for mushing and gushing. We've got a graduation to get to."

Josie smiled, clapping her hands together. "Wait here. Let me grab my cap and gown."

She quickly headed back toward her bedroom and opened the closet to find her freshly dry-cleaned gown hanging. She pulled it over her shoulders, zipped it up, and then adjusted the cap on her head, pinning it against her hair.

Glancing at herself in the mirror again, she found an inner pride bubbling up inside her. She'd worked so hard to become this new version of herself, and seeing the payoff was such a reward. Making an impulse decision, she snapped a photo of herself in the mirror on her iPhone.

She opened the long-dormant Instagram app, reactivated her account, and posted the photo of her in her cap and gown. Then she wrote a caption.

> *You might have noticed I've been gone the last year.*
> *Well, this is what I've been doing.*
> *Welcome the Institute of Culinary Education's latest*
> *graduate—Josie Gray. #readytotaketheworld*
> *#doingthedamnthing #believeinyourself*

The comments began pouring in on her post, and the *likes* immediately started scaling into the thousands. Turning off her notifications, she smiled at the responses she was getting. People were inspired to go back to school for themselves, impressed that she'd given up fame and fortune for education. They were calling her "girl boss" and #bossbabe, and for the first time in her life . . . she felt seen for who she really was.

She wasn't posting sponsored ads and carefully filtered curated content about her reality-star life. She'd just posted an unfiltered selfie in her cap and gown—representing what she really loved and wanted to do with her life.

Spending so much time off social media for the last year had been invigorating for her, and she realized that she had needed the break to find herself again. She'd been living such a staged life for so long, she hadn't even known what it meant to be . . . Josie.

She felt ready now to return to social media but to keep boundaries in place. She wasn't going to let that world overtake her again, and she wasn't going to hide behind filters and sponsors. She was going to be herself and inspire other people to do the same.

It was a new day, and she was damn freaking excited.

CHAPTER TWENTY-TWO

Callan's phone buzzed in his pocket. He debated not looking at it for a moment, but his lunch partner was currently in the bathroom, so he was all alone at the table. Pulling it out, he glanced at the screen.

@JosieGray just posted a new photo.

He lifted his brows. He'd had notifications turned on for Josie's account since they met, but she'd been silent for the past year. And now . . . she was back?

He swiped on the notification, and his phone logged into Instagram and pulled up her picture. It was her. She was wearing a graduation cap and gown that covered most of her body, yet she still looked as sexy and beautiful as he remembered. Her curly locks were sticking out from underneath the cap haphazardly, and she was smiling so brightly, he could practically feel her happiness radiating through the interwebs.

He was glad. He wanted her to be happy and have everything she had dreamed of.

So why did he feel so shitty right now? His heart ached in his chest, and a lump began to form in his throat. He wanted nothing more than to call her, tell her how proud he was of her but also how much he had missed her and needed to see her. Staying away all year had been the hardest thing he'd ever done. She'd asked him for that, and he wanted to respect her wishes, but hundreds of times he'd almost just purchased the plane ticket and said . . . fuck it.

"Sorry about that." A gorgeous blonde sat down across the table from him. Michelle Rae, famous swimsuit model and future star of an upcoming reality show following models around their daily lives, moved her napkin back onto her lap and picked up her glass of wine, taking a sip. "Are we ready to order dessert?"

He looked up from his phone, startled for a moment, and then quickly pushed it back into his pocket. "Uh, yeah. Sure. I was actually looking at the chocolate lava cake. Want to split it?"

"I'd rather do the fruit platter," Michelle commented, pointing to the item on the menu. "My agent will kill me if I'm photographed eating something that fattening."

Callan glanced sideways toward the window of the restaurant, where about a dozen paparazzi were standing on the sidewalk, taking pictures of them. Yes, he was on a date. His first date in over a year. After spending all his time in the cage and winning three championship fights in a row, Callan had found himself to be one of the biggest names in the business. While that was everything for his professional life, it made his personal life take a nosedive.

The only women who surrounded him were groupies, gold diggers, or—like in Michelle's case—a setup from their public relations teams to get them both in the tabloids. She needed publicity for her new show, and he needed to be seen in public with a woman. His PR team was aghast that he'd stayed single so long and was demanding he get out there and make some heads turn.

Frankly, the entire thing was as staged and stupid as he'd been trying to avoid for the last year. Yet, here he was, participating in yet another stunt. Hell, his last official date had been a stunt, too. Even if it had been with a woman where the feelings had been very, very real.

Thinking about that date brought his mind back to Josie's photo in her cap and gown. He couldn't keep his mind off her and couldn't help but start making comparisons in his head between her and Michelle. Josie would have ordered the chocolate lava cake, and she would probably have eaten more than half of it, fighting off his fork with a swing of hers. It was one of the things he'd loved about her.

Love?

The word caught him off guard, and he quickly backtracked in his mind. No, he hadn't been in love with her. How could he have been? They'd only dated for two weeks, and even then, it had been insanely complex. Now, they'd been apart for over a year. Could those feelings really still be there?

He didn't like the answer that was ringing loud in his heart.

"Mmm," Michelle interrupted his thoughts. "This wine is fantastic. Do you want to try some?"

He shook his head, thanking her for the gesture. "Actually, I'm not drinking at the moment. I'm in training for my next fight."

"Right! In Vegas?" she asked.

He nodded, picking at the corner of the dessert menu absentmindedly. "Yeah. Next week."

"That's so exciting. I'd love to come cheer you on," she practically cooed out her words, leaning her elbows on the table in front of her so she could pull closer to him. "Oh, quick.

People magazine just arrived."

She gestured toward a photographer out on the sidewalk. "I'm going to hold your hand and pretend to laugh."

"Uh . . ." He paused, trying to decide what he wanted to do.

"Give me your hand," she urged. "Now . . . smile!"

He reached his hand across the table, and she took it. She then leaned her head back and laughed loudly, smiling wide and turning toward the window so more of her face was in the shot. He plastered a smile on his face, but it was the last thing he wanted to do.

"There. That's good," Michelle said, letting go of his hand and returning to her dessert menu.

The waiter walked up to them, and she ordered the fruit platter for them to share. Callan just said nothing but was mentally ticking down the minutes until he could leave.

"So, tell me," Michelle said. "When's the fight?"

"Friday," he replied, keeping his answers as short and curt as he could.

She pulled her phone out of her clutch and began looking through her calendar. "Good news. I can make it. It'll be tight because of a photo shoot I'm doing that morning, but if it's in the evening, I can get from Los Angeles to Vegas in time."

"It's in the evening," he confirmed. "But you don't have to come. It'll be over in a few minutes. That's a lot of traveling for one fight."

"Nonsense." She waved her hand. "I don't mind one bit. I'll be there with bells on."

Callan just nodded, not sure if he actually wanted her there or not. He knew his publicity team would want her there and that it would be good PR for him, but . . . it felt lackluster now. The connection he'd been hoping to find with this woman was nonexistent, and the reminder of Josie today explained why.

He wasn't over her. But she'd made her intentions clear. She wanted nothing to do with him.

"You know what, Michelle?" he said, deciding that he wasn't going to just keep letting life happen to him. He'd let Josie walk away. He'd let assistants and publicists run his life. He wasn't going to just sit in the passenger seat anymore. Michelle was a wonderful woman, and he respected how hard she worked to make her career take off. Plus, if he was being honest, they had a bit of a past. Sure, it had only been one drunken night together, and he'd certainly never expected it to go anywhere. But he wasn't one to make connections and just leave. He was going to give this woman a chance. If he had to move on, why not with her? "I'd love to have you at the fight with me."

She beamed, thrilled at his invitation. Even though she'd already invited herself.

"Fantastic," she said. "What should I wear?"

"Uh, anything is fine," he replied, not really an expert on women's fashion. "Just as long as you don't mind getting dirty."

"Dirty?" She looked stricken. "What do you mean?"

"Have you ever been to a fight before?" he asked her. "Or seen one on television?"

She shook her head. "No, but I'm excited to try it out!"

He loved her enthusiasm and willingness to take on the world, but he was definitely worried she'd bitten off more than she could chew. "There will be a lot of sweat . . . and blood."

"Blood?" She gasped. "Seriously? I thought it was mostly staged?"

Callan lifted one brow, trying to gauge if she really thought that or not. "I think you're thinking of pageant wrestling... some of which is definitely staged. But I'm a mixed martial artist fighter. We... we do the damn thing."

"Oh." She lifted her chin slightly, digesting this new information. "Wow. That's... that's kind of hot."

He laughed at her candor. Maybe she wasn't all there upstairs, but the woman was humorous. "Well, thank you. I guess."

"I'll be prepared for blood and guts." She set her lips in a thin line. "Bring it on."

"Slow down," he cautioned, still chuckling. "You shouldn't be seeing anyone's guts. Something will have really gone wrong if that happens."

She looked relieved. "Okay. Good."

The waiter delivered the fruit platter, placing it on the table. "Would you like some more wine, ma'am?" he asked Michelle.

Michelle nodded. "Yes, please."

That was her fourth glass of wine, but he was trying his best not to judge. It wasn't his business how much she drank, even though it made him a little nervous. He didn't really feel in the mood to take care of a drunk woman today. He would, of course, but he wouldn't enjoy it. That was for damn sure.

"So, Cal," Michelle started. "Tell me. Do you live far from here?"

"No," he replied. "I'm about two miles northwest. Right on the beach in Malibu."

She nodded slowly, pursing her lips. "Interesting. What a beautiful view you must have."

"It is pretty incredible," he agreed. He loved living in the Los Angeles area, but he'd found himself traveling so much lately that he was rarely home. He was considering selling and moving his permanent location to Las Vegas to be closer to the training center and where most of his matches were. The commute back and forth was just getting tiring.

"I'd love to . . . to see it. You know, after lunch?" Michelle's suggestive tone left no room for interpretation. It was clear what she was asking, and part of him wanted to say yes. He wanted to just bury himself inside her and forget all about his life, about the woman who'd left him and torn his heart to pieces.

But . . . Michelle wasn't Josie. It was really that simple.

"Not today," he replied, avoiding making direct eye contact with her as he placed his napkin on the table. "Actually, I have to get running. I have an important meeting to get to."

Not really a lie—he *was* meeting with his trainer in an hour.

"Do you ever think about . . . about that night we had together?" Michelle asked.

Callan lifted his head, gazing into her eyes for a moment, trying to remember the feelings he'd had that night weeks ago when they'd hooked up after a drunken night at the club. But . . . he couldn't pull any emotions out. He felt nothing.

It had been a one-night stand that he instantly regretted, and as soon as his assistant had found out about it, it had landed him in this situation.

"Sure, I think about it," he lied to her, not wanting to hurt her feelings.

"Maybe Friday night . . . we can have a repeat of that night. It's been a while," she mused.

"Chances are I'll be pretty exhausted after the fight," he said, deflecting her advance. It was pretty true, though. After a championship fight, all he usually wanted to do was rest and recoup. Not to mention getting medical attention for whatever scrapes and breaks he'd received in the cage.

"That's okay. I'll see you on Friday, then?" she asked.

He nodded as he handed the waiter his credit card. "Yeah. I'll be there."

After signing the bill, he stood up and came around to Michelle's side of the table. He offered her a hug, which she took wholeheartedly, embracing him tightly. All the while, she was making sure the cameras caught her every move and saw the two of them locked together.

Letting go, Callan said his goodbyes and then headed out the door. He tried to swallow the feeling of dread in his stomach that told him he was making a mistake . . . that this wasn't what he really wanted.

That this wasn't Josie.

CHAPTER TWENTY-THREE

Fan-freaking-tastic.

The moment Josie stepped off the plane in Las Vegas and jumped into her Lyft to head toward her brother's house, she saw Callan's handsome face staring back at her.

Well, to be more clear, it was a picture of his face on a giant billboard towering above her as they drove. According to the information on the sign, he was starring in yet another championship fight in Vegas this Friday.

So, they were both in Vegas for the week. She was here for an interview with Michael Rockport, and he was here for another fight that he was certainly going to win. He'd won every fight he'd been in over the last year. Not that she'd been stalking him or anything...

She just liked to keep up-to-date on his career and what he was going through. Admittedly, she also followed him online to see what the latest gossip was about his life. Thankfully, he seemed to not really have much of a life. Not that she was hoping he was still single, but...

Okay, so she kind of hoped he was.

Sighing, she turned away from the billboard and focused on the headrest of the passenger seat in front of her. Glancing down, she noticed some magazines stuffed in the back pocket of the front seat. Pulling out the latest copy of *OK!* magazine, she surveyed the cover.

Latest Kardashian meltdown—caught on tape! Looked promising.

Brad Pitt caught with his pants down. That was definitely a lie.

MMA star Callan Walsh cozies up to swimsuit model. Her breath caught in her throat. *Excuse me?*

She immediately turned to the page for the story on the cover. Sure enough, there were large photos of Callan having lunch with a gorgeous blonde in a tight spandex dress that hugged every inch of her nonexistent curves. Except for her giant tits. Those were definitely paid for.

Jealousy bubbled up in her stomach, and she tried to push it away. Why did she even care? They hadn't been together in over a year, and when they had been together, it was for two weeks. Barely enough time for anything to happen.

Except something had happened.

Her heart had gotten involved.

Josie took in the photos in front of her. Callan was smiling at the laughing swimsuit model, and they were holding hands. They looked . . . happy. She hadn't expected him to stay single forever, but it stung nonetheless to see it in front of her face.

Tucking the magazine back into the pocket of the seat in front of her, she tried to push the entire thing out of her mind. She wasn't in town to think about Callan. She'd left him for a reason—to pursue her career.

That was what she was doing here.

She pulled out her phone and opened it to the notes section. She reread the talking points and interview tips that she had been practicing for the last few days in preparation for today. Overall, she felt very ready for this interview and was certain she was going to knock it out of the park.

In just the first week since her graduation, she'd gotten three job offers to places she'd applied and from one place that had sought her out from her graduating class. However, one job was in Texas and the other two were in New York City. As much as she loved the city—and these jobs were truly great opportunities—it wasn't her home, and they weren't Michael Rockport.

Just driving the back roads from the airport toward the strip where her brother now lived full-time in a hotel penthouse, she couldn't help but take in all the sights of the city she loved so much. Vegas was in her blood. It was a part of her, and she couldn't believe that she'd ever left. Sure, it had been an amazing opportunity, and she'd needed the break from her family and that whole world. But now? Now things were different. She was ready to come home. She was ready to settle down into a life she'd always dreamed of.

If only it would have her.

Her Lyft pulled up to the hotel a few minutes later, and Josie thanked the driver as he opened the door for her and she stepped out. A lone paparazzo hanging out on the sidewalk in front of the hotel snapped her picture and tried calling out to her, but she ignored him and ducked inside quickly.

"Hi. I'm here to see Michael Rockport," she said to the restaurant manager after she'd finally located her in the bustling restaurant tucked away inside the Venetian Hotel.

"Your name?" the woman asked, smiling brightly.

"Josie Gray," she replied.

"I'll let him know you're here. Why don't you take a seat at the bar and help yourself to a cocktail while you wait—complimentary, of course."

"Thank you." Josie made her way over to the bar and hopped up on one of the luxurious high-top chairs.

The bartender came over and asked her what she'd liked to drink.

"Vodka and soda."

He quickly brought her drink and then left her there alone to pass her time as she sipped on the edge of her glass. She busied herself playing with her phone while she waited, and about fifteen minutes went by before she heard a familiar voice greeting her.

"Ms. Gray," Rockport called out to her, walking up to her at the bar. "It's so lovely to see you again. It's been, what, a year now?"

She nodded her head, quickly standing and extending her hand to the celebrity chef. "A little over that, actually."

"Well, I was just thrilled when I got a call from your brother that you're open for a job. I've been following your progress at ICE in New York, and I must say—I'm impressed."

"Thank you so much," she quickly responded, feeling more nervous at the praise than grateful.

"Come, let me give you a tour of the restaurant, and then we'll meet in my office for a little bit." He gestured for her to follow him, so she did.

Rockport showed her around the main dining area and then more carefully took her through the kitchen, explaining every station to her and introducing her to everyone who worked there. It was overwhelming and exciting, but she couldn't have been more grateful for the opportunity to see a real Vegas kitchen in full swing.

"Do you have any questions?" Rockport asked her as they entered his office. It was large and expansive, a floor up from the dining room beneath it.

"My only question is when can I start?" she said confidently.

Rockport laughed, his head tipping backward as his belly

jiggled. "You're eager. I like that."

"Thank you."

"I'll be honest," he started. "I've already looked over your résumé, done my research, and your teachers all speak very highly of you. I'd like you to whip up one dish for me, and if everything goes smoothly, I'll have the contracts drawn up immediately."

Josie clapped her hands together. "I'd love that. What would you like me to cook?"

"I'll leave that up to you, but I'm going to throw in a mystery ingredient for you to use." He lifted one brow, a small smirk on his face.

That was just like what he did on his show—giving contestants a mystery ingredient to incorporate into their dishes and make it the star. It was always something slightly odd or offbeat, but she loved the concept.

"I would be more than happy to do that. What's the ingredient?"

"Chickpeas," he said. "We're a Mediterranean-fusion restaurant, so I thought it seemed fitting. You can go on into the kitchen and get started. I'll grab you an extra chef's coat. Oh, and Josie? You have twenty minutes."

Ideas immediately started to flood Josie's brain as excitement coursed through her at the prospect. She headed to the kitchen, and after putting on a borrowed chef's coat, she began rummaging through the fridge and pantry to see what types of ingredients she could throw together.

Quickly, she concocted a plan and pulled together the necessary items. Rockport had set her up at her own station in the corner so she was out of the way of the other people in the kitchen preparing lunch for the diners. Deciding to stick with the theme of the restaurant, Josie prepared a vegan spanakopita, swapping out the feta cheese for a chickpea and tahini mixture that perfectly complemented the phyllo dough and spinach.

She was cutting it close to the wire, almost hitting the twenty-minute mark, but she managed to make it just in time, pulling out a small baking dish perfect for individual portions from the oven. Plating it on a pristine white ceramic, she topped it with a few garnishes and then walked it back up to the office where she'd be meeting Michael Rockport again.

"Ah, Josie. You're all done?" he asked her as she entered, holding the dish in one hand with a kitchen rag to keep her hand from burning. "What have you got?"

"Chef, I've made you a vegan spanakopita featuring chickpeas and tahini." She placed the dish in front of him and stepped back, her chest puffing up slightly at the pride she was feeling. She'd put her all into this dish, and it was a damn fine piece of culinary work.

Rockport took the fork from the side of his plate and dug it into the food, brought it to his mouth, and took his time savoring the bite. He returned his fork to the spanakopita and took a second bite, chewing just as carefully. Finally, he laid the fork down and turned his attention to her.

"Well, Josie." He shook his head. "This might be better than regular spanakopita. You've done a phenomenal job."

She beamed. "Thank you, Chef."

"I'd say it's safe to assume you'll be receiving a contract in your email very shortly." Rockport stood and extended a hand to her. "Welcome aboard, Ms. Gray."

CHAPTER TWENTY-FOUR

It had been a long time since she'd come to O'Hannigan's Bar & Grill. In fact, the last time Josie had walked through these doors had been over a year ago, when she'd first met Callan. She wasn't sure what it was about tonight, but she was feeling... nostalgic.

Seating herself at the bar, she ordered a vodka soda from the bartender and immediately took a sip when he brought it to her. Nerves settled in her belly as she thought of everything happening tomorrow. It was her first shift as sous chef at Niro's. Even though she'd only interviewed for the job three days ago, the hiring process had gone fast. They'd processed her paperwork and gotten her in the door immediately. They'd even given her a huge signing bonus to help her find a place to live in Vegas and move all her stuff from New York City. She was still staying in her brother's hotel at the moment, but she planned to find a place as soon as she had the time. Tomorrow was her first day shadowing the head chef at Niro's, and she couldn't be more excited.

Apparently, the head chef was retiring in the next year, so Rockport's plan was to have her train under him and then take over as head chef once he retired. It was a lot for a brand-new chef on the scene, but he seemed convinced she could do it.

And hell, she wanted it. Badly.

There was nothing she would love more than to run her own kitchen—and in one of the best restaurants on the Las

Vegas strip? It was nothing short of a dream come true.

"Nice seeing you here," a familiar voice interrupted her thoughts.

Josie turned around to see Callan Walsh standing behind her. He was dressed in a suit and looked like he'd just come from a fancy event—way out of the league of a dive bar like O'Hannigan's. But damn, it fit him perfectly. She could still see every bulge of his muscular arms under the jacket, and the way his hair was slicked back, pulled into a tight ponytail . . . he just looked rugged.

She'd almost forgotten how handsome he was in person. Sure, he'd looked hot as hell in the photographs she'd seen, but it was nothing compared to the real thing.

"Callan . . ." His name left her lips slowly, almost like a breath being exhaled. She was startled to see him in person . . . and here? Their spot.

"Josie," he greeted her in turn. "Mind if I sit here?"

He gestured to the stool beside her. She nodded that it was fine, and he pulled out the stool and sat.

"It's been a while," he said quietly. "How are you?"

"I-I'm good," she said, stumbling over her words. "How have you been?"

He tilted his chin down slightly, as if he didn't know how he was going to respond. When his eyes rose back to hers, they were filled with . . . was it sorrow? She sensed a sadness behind him that she couldn't quite put her finger on.

"I've been okay," he said. "You look amazing."

His words rang sincere, and the way his eyes raked over her body . . . it gave her the best kind of chills.

A heavy silence hung over them for a moment as she tried to think of something to say instead of just staring at him and his perfect jawline.

"I heard you have a fight tomorrow," she said finally, trying to make conversation. Small talk was the devil. "And a new girlfriend. Congratulations."

"Thank you. I'm looking forward to the match tomorrow. And Michelle isn't exactly my girlfriend," he quickly clarified. "We have just been out a few times."

"Oh." That was interesting. Then again, tabloids were known for fabricating the truth. "Well, still, congratulations on everything."

"I appreciate that. Are you coming to the match?"

He looked eager, hopeful. She hated to dash it, but she was going to be in the kitchen tomorrow for the first time. She shook her head, looking down at her glass.

"No. I have to work," she explained and then took a sip from her drink. Then another. Honestly, she'd need a second drink to get through this conversation without throwing herself at him. Just being this close to him . . . it was lighting up every cell in her body. She felt like she was on fire just from his proximity, and she wanted to both run away and jump him at the same time.

"Work?" He lifted his brow. "Here? In Vegas?"

She nodded, putting aside her feelings for a moment to excitedly talk about her new job. "At Niro's, actually. Rockport hired me full-time."

"That's absolutely amazing," he replied. "You've always wanted that."

"It's a dream come true."

"I saw that you graduated ICE," he continued. "Looks like I should be congratulating you. A new degree and a new job—you're killing it."

Heat pumped into her cheeks at the compliment. "Thank you."

They were quiet for a moment. Again. Awkwardness seemed to be the theme of the evening, and she didn't like it. *Have I completely blown things with him?* Things had once been so effortless between them, and now it was like pulling teeth to figure out what to say.

"Well, I should get going," she finally said, finishing off the last of her drink and pulling a few bills out of her clutch to place on the bar.

"Keep your money," he told her, motioning to the bartender. "This one's on me."

"Oh. Thanks." She slid the cash back into her clutch. "That's very sweet of you. Well . . . bye."

In the most awkward moment of the century, she turned on her heels and walked out of the bar. Stopping at the curb, she mentally kicked herself for the incredibly awful way that interaction had gone. Why hadn't she said what she was really feeling? Why hadn't she asked him back to her hotel? Not that she really could, since she was living with her brother. Fuck. Why hadn't she just told him that she hadn't stopped thinking about him for over a year and she wanted nothing more than to be in his arms again?

"I haven't stopped thinking about you, you know," Callan's voice came from behind her, catching her off guard in her thoughts as she was mentally berating herself.

She turned slowly to face him, hoping she had really heard what she thought she'd heard.

"Is that so?" she replied, trying to keep her voice as level as possible.

He nodded, his hands in his suit pockets as he approached her. They were alone, only the dull noise from the inside of the bar trickling through the doors.

"What was that in there?" he asked her, gesturing back behind them toward the bar. "Because that wasn't us."

She felt some of the tension break between them. He took her hand and squeezed it.

"I don't know," she said. "I feel ... I feel nervous around you."

"Why?" He pushed her for an answer she wasn't sure she was ready to give.

But life was about taking chances and putting your heart on the line when the payoff could be forever.

"Because ..." she started. "Because I haven't been able to stop thinking about you either."

As hard as it was to admit that, the truth felt freeing. There had once been a time where she felt like she could tell Callan anything ... and she wanted to get back to that. She wanted to remind herself of what they had, what they could be.

His eyes darkened, hooding as he looked down at her with a fire she wasn't sure she'd ever be able to extinguish. "Jos ..."

She swallowed hard, loving the way he said her nickname.

"Go on a date with me."

"What?" She hadn't expected that from him.

"Go on a date with me," he repeated. "A real date this time. Let's see if what we think is here ... is really here. Let's give this a real shot this time. Slow and steady."

She paused for a moment, unsure how to respond. It was everything she'd been wanting to hear, but could she get involved with a man who was leaving as soon as his fight was over?

"When?" she asked.

"Tomorrow, after your shift."

"You're going to be just coming off a fight. You'll be exhausted."

"All right. Then Saturday." He shrugged his shoulders as if he didn't care what day they went out, as if all he wanted was to see her. "I'll be here through Sunday night, so anytime."

She swallowed at the confirmation that, yes, he was leaving. But she couldn't say no. Not to him.

"Okay," she finally replied. "Saturday."

"Is your number still the same?" He lifted one brow as he gazed at her.

She nodded. "It is."

"Great. I'll text you the details." He motioned to a black car that was pulling up. "In the meantime, take my car home."

"I can order a Lyft," she immediately responded, feeling bad about the idea of taking his ride.

"I wasn't asking," he told her. "You're a lot safer with my driver. He can come back and get me later."

She paused for a moment, realizing that she didn't want to say no . . . again. What was it about him that made her never want to say anything other than yes?

"Okay, but under one condition . . ." She trailed off, rubbing her hand against her opposite arm. "You share the ride with me. Drop me off and then go home. I'm not taking your ride from you."

He seemed appeased by that arrangement and nodded. "Fair enough. Let's go."

The driver parked the car at the curb and came around to open the door for them.

"We're making an extra stop," Callan told his driver.

"Not a problem," the man replied. He turned to Josie next. "Welcome, young lady."

"Thank you." She took his hand as he helped her into the back seat of the car.

Callan climbed in after her and sat next to her. "Where are you staying?" he asked.

"With Xavier," she admitted reluctantly, feeling slightly embarrassed at her lack of independence. She gave Callan the address, and he relayed it to the driver. "It's only temporary until all my stuff is delivered. I just started this job, and it was rapid on-boarding."

"Can you do me a favor?" Callan angled his body to face hers.

"Uh . . . sure."

"For the rest of this ride, can we not talk about work? Or our home life? All those things that tore us apart a year ago? It's just you and me . . . here and now."

She swallowed hard, trying to ease her racing heart. It felt like it was pounding against her ribcage so hard, it might burst through. "I'm sure I can manage that."

Callan reached out a hand toward her face, pushing back a curly lock of hair off her cheek. They didn't say anything for a few moments and just stared at each other instead.

She finally took a deep breath and slowly exhaled. It was all just too much, and she wasn't sure she could handle another moment. Her body felt like it was on fire anytime she was around him, and all she could think about was how his lips had felt on hers a year ago.

An entire year . . .

She couldn't believe that much time had passed since they'd been together, because when she thought of their brief fling, it felt like yesterday.

Deciding to take life by the horns, Josie pushed up on her feet and turned her body toward him, facing him as she climbed onto his lap. She straddled him with her legs on either side of his, her chest to his as she circled her arms around the back of his neck.

"Kiss me," she instructed him, nearly panting at the thought.

He didn't need more coaxing than that. Callan wrapped his arms around her back and pulled her flush against him. His lips were on hers in seconds, and every tension in her body released. She melted into his arms, their kiss slow and lingering. His tongue slid past her lips, exploring her as she parted for him, giving him every bit of herself.

If she'd been wearing a skirt, she had no doubt that she'd slide him inside her right then and there. She was certainly ready for him. But unfortunately, she'd chosen to wear skinny jeans today, and there was no way she was managing to get those off in the back of a moving car.

It seemed like only seconds had gone by since they'd started kissing, yet she felt the car coming to a stop. Glancing up, she recognized the entrance to the hotel where Xavier lived.

Callan grinned, biting the edge of his lip as he stared back at her with hooded eyes. "Good night, Jos," he said, helping her slide back to the seat and right herself. "Sleep well before your big day tomorrow."

"Thank you," she replied. "You too."

She stepped out of the car and turned to look back at him. Callan opened the window and gave her a slight nod of his head. She wanted to ask him to come in with her, spend the night cuddling together . . . but she lived with her brother.

While Xavier had never expressed anything negative to her, she wasn't entirely sure her brother was Callan's biggest fan after his loss to him last year. It would be disastrous if

Xavier woke up and found him here.

Sighing, Josie gave Callan a small wave and then turned and headed back into the hotel. There was no doubt in her mind that she would barely sleep a wink tonight.

She had no idea what tomorrow had in store for her . . .

CHAPTER TWENTY-FIVE

Callan's vision blurred, sight slowly returning to him as he tried to place where he was and what was happening. He was staring up at a ceiling—black piping covering every inch with banners and flags hanging from them. Recognition hit him as he realized...

I'm in the arena!

Quickly, he tried to scramble to his feet to avoid his opponent getting the best of him again, but he couldn't lift his arm. It was pinned beneath him, and despite his best efforts, he couldn't sit up and free himself.

Blood gushed down the side of his face, and he wanted to wipe it away but couldn't. The metallic taste settled on his tongue, and his mouth guard suddenly felt like it was going to choke him.

"Get up!" he heard Ferguson yelling in the background as his hearing went from a dull roar to parsing out individual voices.

Someone was counting.

Someone else was calling out his name.

People were screaming and cheering...some were even booing.

He turned his head sideways to see his opponent walking in circles around the cage with his hands up in the air.

And that was the last thing he saw before everything went black.

CHAPTER TWENTY-SIX

Her first shift had been anything but easy. The speed at which the kitchen moved was faster than anything she had experienced before. Dishes were going out left and right, and each one had to be perfect. No mistakes. This was a five-star restaurant in the middle of the Las Vegas strip.

There was no room for error.

"Behind!" called out a kitchen staff member as he walked behind her in the kitchen, heading back to his station.

Josie moved out of the way and returned her focus to the dish she was working on. Wiping the spills and splashes off the side of the dish, she put it up under the warmer and called out the order number. A waiter immediately appeared and loaded the plate onto a tray, leaving the kitchen moments later.

She smiled, loving the powerful, energizing feeling of being a chef. It was truly everything she'd been working toward and had hoped for. But damn, it wasn't easy. She'd spent the early part of the afternoon doing inventory before it had been time to hit the grill—and she still had to finish that up after the dinner rush.

"Josie?" Rockport called out, entering the kitchen. He bent down, looking through the metal shelving to find her. Locating her at her station, he came closer. "Josie, can I talk to you for a second?"

Her stomach dropped. Had she fucked up already?

"Sure," she replied quickly, trying to hide the fact that she was nervous as hell. "Be right out."

She finished up the plate she was working on, serving it up under the warmer and then walking down to the end of the station and coming around to the plating section, where Rockport was.

He was holding a tablet but gestured for her to follow him. They walked over to a corner of the kitchen before he stopped and turned to face her.

"I know you've been busy working, so I'm guessing you haven't seen this," Rockport began. "I thought ... well, I don't know. Maybe you should."

"What is it?" Nerves exploded tenfold in her stomach at his words.

He turned the tablet to face her. It was set to a local sports channel and was paused. He pressed play.

A sportscaster came on the screen with the following caption underneath: *MMA Legend knocked out in the cage.*

"That's right, folks. The day has come. The beast has fallen. MMA Legend Callan Walsh lost tonight's championship fight to Ruiz Salazar in an incredible knockout scene."

An instant replay video of the event began to play. Sure enough, there was Callan—blood all over his face—as his opponent's fist decked him right in the jaw. He went down, lights out, almost immediately. Salazar jumped on him and kept punching, even though he was down. The ref had to pull him off and wrangle him to the side as medics rushed in to take care of Callan.

"Are you okay?" Rockport asked.

She hadn't realized until he pointed it out, but she'd started crying. Tears streamed down her cheeks as fear filled her belly at the thought of Callan in real danger. She tried to respond to reassure her boss that she was fine, but she couldn't talk.

"Listen," Rockport began, turning off the tablet and tucking it under his arm. "Walsh is a good friend of mine. I don't usually let people leave early—especially in the middle of the dinner shift and especially not on their first day—but... someone needs to be with him. The way he's been talking about you for the last year? I think it should be you."

He'd been talking about her to his friends? Her heart warmed at the thought, but not enough to eclipse the terror she was feeling.

Quickly, she nodded and thanked him. Taking off her hairnet, she tossed it into the garbage and headed for the door. She had no time to waste if she was going to find Callan and be by his side. The problem was... she didn't know how to locate him.

She had an idea as she walked—or ran—out to her car. She pulled out her phone and dialed her brother's number.

"Xav?"

He made a slight groaning sound, as if she'd just awoken him from sleeping. It was only ten o'clock, but her brother had early nights these days. He wasn't the partier he'd once been, that was for sure.

"What's happening?" he replied. "Everything okay?"

She shook her head, even though he couldn't see her. "I need a favor."

"Does this have anything to do with tonight's fight?" Xavier seemed to already know before she'd even said anything.

"I need to see him, Xav," she responded. "I need to know he's okay."

"All right. I got you." Xavier paused for a moment,

probably thinking over their options. "Okay, I'll call his trainer, Ferguson. Give me a few minutes. I'll locate him."

"Xav?"

"Yeah?"

She put a hand to her chest. "Thank you."

"Anytime, baby sis." He hung up the phone.

She climbed into her car and started heading in the direction of the arena. Minutes later, she received a text message notification. Waiting until she got to a red light, she glanced down at her phone and read the news from Xavier.

He was airlifted to Los Angeles General.
Fergie put you on the list to see him.

He was in Los Angeles? What the hell? She didn't even need to debate it in her mind. She plugged the address into her phone's GPS and started the long drive from Vegas to LA.

All that mattered was that she got to him in time . . .

CHAPTER TWENTY-SEVEN

Hospital chairs were incredibly uncomfortable. One would think that with everything people visiting a hospital had to deal with, they would at least try to keep people's asses from falling asleep in hard plastic chairs.

Josie readjusted herself, trying to find a comfortable position. She was seated in a small chair next to Callan's bedside. It was the middle of the night, and he was still sleeping. Thankfully, the nurses had let her in even though it wasn't visiting hours.

Sure, she'd had to lie and tell them she was his wife.

But what he didn't know wouldn't hurt him.

Cracking her neck from side to side, she stretched her arms over her head. Damn, she was stiff from driving so far and then sitting in this shitty chair.

A nurse she hadn't seen before walked in. They must have just switched shifts.

"Are you Mrs. Walsh?" the nurse asked, a softness in her voice as she smiled at Josie.

Josie nodded. "I am."

"Great. I'm Rebecca. I'll be the day nurse for the morning. I'm going to write my name and call number on the board over here so you can just reach me on that phone over there whenever you need me," she explained. "I'm going to take his vitals really quickly and then get out of your hair."

"Okay." Josie watched the woman busy herself with the different tasks.

A few minutes later, she left, and the room was quiet again.

"Mrs. Walsh, huh?" Callan angled his head to face her.

Apparently, he'd been awake the entire time.

The heat of a blush crept into her cheeks and bloomed across her face. "Uh..."

"It's okay," he replied, saving her from coming up with some lame excuse as to why she'd been called that. "I kind of like the sound of it."

She chuckled lightly. "It's not the worst thing I've ever been called," she teased.

He stared at her for a moment. Finally, he spoke. "What are you doing here, Jos?"

Fidgeting with her hands in her lap, she replayed the moment in her mind when she'd seen the video. All the blood. Callan on the floor. A lump began to form in her throat as she remembered the scene. "I—I saw the fight. Well, a video of the fight."

He didn't respond, letting her finish what she wanted to say.

"I had to come make sure you were okay," she finished. "I needed to be here with you."

"What about your job?" he asked, and she noticed there was a look of guilt crossing his expression.

She quickly shook her head. "They're fine with me being here. Everything is fine."

He looked relieved, letting out a big exhale of air. "Well... good. Still, I'm sorry you had to see me like this."

"I'm not," she replied. "It's kind of humbling seeing this new side of you."

"The loser side?" He lifted one brow to look at her, then winced, as he must have realized his brow had stitches in it.

"You're not a loser." She reached out and took his hand in both of hers. "You just lost one fight. There will be others."

"Yeah . . . epic way to go down, though." He seemed wistful, a longing look in his eyes as he angled his body to face her.

"There will be other fights. I heard your trainer talking about the appeal of a comeback and how that would boost your image . . ." She tried to assuage him, knowing he was feeling pretty shitty at the moment. "Believe me, after everything my brother has gone through, yet he still comes out on top? You will too."

"How is Gray doing?" Callan asked. "Haven't heard much from him on the circuit lately."

"His focus has shifted a lot. He's doing really well."

Callan nodded and then lifted the blanket and gestured for her to come join him in the bed.

She paused for a moment because she was scared of hurting him, but the thought of being curled up in his arms was just too appealing. Carefully, she climbed into bed next to him and laid her head on his shoulder.

His arm circled around her back and pulled her even tighter against him. "Sorry, but I think I'm going to miss our date," he said quietly. "I need to make it up to you."

She smiled slightly, just the corners of her lips lifting. "I'll hold you to that."

"How long are you in Los Angeles for?" he asked her.

Technically, she had to be at work on Tuesday, but that did give her the weekend to spend here if she wanted. She didn't want to overstay her welcome, however, so she decided to stay vague.

"A few days," she explained. "I'm booking a room at the hotel down the street from here so I can be close."

"What? That's ridiculous. You can stay at my house. Keys are in my pants pocket over in that bag of clothes. Plus, I'll be able to go home later today or tomorrow if they determine the concussion wasn't too severe."

She glanced toward the hospital bag that he was pointing to. "Really?"

He nodded. "Of course. Someone needs to water the plants."

Josie laughed. "I see. Just using me to do your chores."

"I'll need a detailed report, too. Got to make sure the plants are properly taken care of."

"Do you even have plants?" she asked, skeptical.

Callan shook his head, his telltale smirk on his lips. "Plastic ones."

"You're ridiculous," she responded, closing her eyes and feeling the pull of sleep.

Being in the bed was more comfortable than the hospital chair—and having his arms around her? Added bonus.

"Uh, Mr. and... Mrs. Walsh?" Nurse Rebecca had returned to the room. She looked incredibly nervous, her brows pulled together and her hands fidgeting in front of her. "Uh, can I speak to Mr. Walsh alone for a moment?"

Callan frowned. "Anything you say to me you can say to my wife."

"Your fucking *wife*?" A shrill voice came from behind Rebecca, and a tall, modelesque woman with platinum-blond hair stepped around the nurse. "You might have mentioned the fact that you have a *wife* when we were going out on dates."

Josie immediately recognized the woman as the one from the tabloids who Callan had been seen out on a few dates with. She quickly sat up and scrambled off the bed, as if she'd been caught doing something wrong. Though ... had she? Last she'd spoken to Callan at O'Hannigan's, he'd made it seem that it was nothing serious.

"Michelle..." Callan put his hand out, as if to tell her to stop. He then turned his attention to the nurse. "Can we have privacy for a moment?"

"Of course." Rebecca looked more than thrilled to get out of the room and practically ran to the exit.

"Well?" Michelle asked, crossing her arms over her chest and tapping her foot. "Do you care to explain why you'd embarrass me like this?"

"Josie and I are not really married," he assured the woman.

Josie tried not to be offended at that remark—after all, it was the truth. However, she couldn't help but feel slighted at the dismissal. She stood awkwardly to the side, trying to figure out what to do with herself. She wanted to follow Rebecca and run right out of the room, but then part of her wanted to stay and fight for the man she loved.

Loved?

The word caught her off guard, and she swallowed hard, trying to push away the feelings. She couldn't afford to let her heart run away from her right now—not when the man in question might have a girlfriend.

"Okay..." Michelle replied, letting her arms fall to her sides. "Then what is going on? Because I'm really confused."

"Michelle, I've really enjoyed going out with you the last few times, but ... it was set up by our public relations teams, as you know. It wasn't ... it wasn't real."

The supermodel's bottom lip quivered slightly. "But ... I came to your fight."

"You also waited until the next morning to check in on me

at the hospital," he pointed out.

Josie grimaced because now everything felt awkward as hell.

Michelle lifted her chin slightly. "I have a very strict sleep schedule. You know that. My skin can't handle sleeping in a hospital chair overnight."

He didn't reply to that but just waited.

"And who are *you*?" Michelle turned her attention to Josie now. "I've never seen you before."

"Uh . . . I'm nobody," Josie quickly assured her. "Just an old friend."

Callan cut his eyes to her, an annoyed look on his face. "She's not just an old friend. She's the woman I love. The woman I'm going to marry."

Holy. Fucking. Shit.

An awkward silence filled the room as both women tried to process what he'd just said.

"Well." Michelle crossed her arms over her chest again. "I guess that answers that. Call me when this whole thing blows up in your face."

"Goodbye, Michelle," he responded, excusing her.

Her nostrils flared and she lifted her chin in defiance, but she didn't respond. Instead, she just turned and walked out of the hospital room, heels clicking sharply against the polished floor.

Josie stared after her, trying to figure out what to say . . . or how to absorb everything that had just happened.

"Jos," Callan called to her, his hand raised and motioning for her to return to the bed.

She paused for a minute, unsure of what to do. Finally, she stepped closer but then stopped. "Callan . . . I don't know what to say right now."

"Say you'll get in this bed and cuddle with me," he replied.

"Am I . . . am I the other woman?" she asked. "Did I just break up a happy relationship?"

Callan slowly shook his head and then winced. His head must still hurt from his injuries. "Not even in the slightest. Were Michelle and I seeing each other? Yes. Was it all staged for the paparazzi to help further both of our careers? Also, yes. There were no real feelings there. No real expectations. Frankly, I'm not even sure why she was upset. She never indicated that she wanted more than a publicity stunt."

Josie could kind of see that. The woman had definitely come across as very focused on image. Knowing what she did know about Callan, she couldn't really imagine him with someone who lacked that much depth.

"Plus," he reminded her, "you're the one who called yourself my wife."

She grinned slightly at that. "The poor nurse . . ."

Callan laughed. "Oh, my God. She must be traumatized."

Josie crawled back into bed with him and wrapped her arm around his chest. "Should we talk about everything else you said?"

She's the woman I'm going to marry.

"We can," he replied. "I don't take back any of it. I'm going to marry you one day, Josie Gray."

Excitement skittered through her veins at the thought of it.

"And Josie . . ." he continued. "I do love you. I am *in* love with you. You showing up here at the hospital to make sure I'm okay even when you live so far away? That only confirmed it for me. I know without a doubt now . . . I am, and maybe have been for a longer time than I realized, absolutely head-over-heels in love with you."

"Callan . . ." she began, her breath coming fast and hard as panic began to rise in her.

"You don't have to say it back," he interrupted. "I just wanted you to know. I'm in this. I'm not going anywhere. You pushed me away last year, and I let you. That was a mistake I'm not making again."

Her heart pounded in her chest. Anxiety bloomed in her stomach, fluttering butterflies flying wild. She couldn't deny that she'd thought the same things, that she was even *feeling* the same things . . . but she couldn't seem to say it out loud.

At least not yet.

She needed to know this was real. She needed to know he wasn't going anywhere. But, more importantly, she needed to know she wasn't going to run either. Because right now? All she wanted to do was race out of this room and be as far away as possible.

Because if her heart broke again . . .

She wasn't sure she'd survive it.

CHAPTER TWENTY-EIGHT

"I'd say you look pretty distinguished," Josie said behind Callan as he looked at himself in the mirror. "The scars really add to your features."

He turned around to give her a weird face—his nose scrunched up as if he didn't believe a word she was saying. "You're blowing smoke up my ass now."

She shook her head and then reached out and ran a hand across the line of his jaw. "I'm not. It's rugged. It'll just make you look even tougher in the cage."

He glanced back at the mirror, surveying his reflection. He had a bandage covering the stitches that cut right through his brow and a dark bruise across his cheekbone that was still swollen. His bottom lip was split but healing, and he could still taste the blood from the fight whenever he thought about it.

It had felt embarrassing to lose so badly in the championship. He'd won it last year and come in cocky, fully expecting to beat his opponent again like it was nothing. He hadn't prepared as well as he'd needed to, and for that, he took full responsibility.

He wasn't a vain person, and his appearance had never mattered that much to him, but something about the new bruises and scars made a new feeling of self-consciousness begin to bloom in him. Maybe because he'd spent the last two days with Josie, whose dark skin was absolutely flawless and who had cheekbones that could cut diamonds.

"Come on," she urged him, pulling on his arm. "Let's go to bed. I have an early drive in the morning."

The reminder struck him like a baseball bat out of nowhere. It had been such a short time—again—but he'd gotten accustomed to her being in his home. The idea of her leaving . . . well, it felt like last year all over again.

After his admission in the hospital room, the stakes seemed even higher. He'd put his entire self out there only to be left hanging. She hadn't responded with her feelings. She hadn't assured him that she'd stay. She hadn't given an inch.

And now she was leaving for Vegas.

He'd known it was coming. Hell, she had a life to go back to. A brand-new job that she'd earned. He wasn't going to stand in the way of that.

But that didn't mean he was going to let her drop out of his life either.

"Do you have to go?" he asked, following her to the bedroom hand-in-hand.

She glanced up at him, squeezing his hand. "It's where my new job is. I can't exactly quit now."

Of course that was true. Hell, he'd be pissed at her if she quit just to follow him to Los Angeles. He didn't want to disrupt her life, even though selfishly he wanted to keep her all for himself.

"Callan?" she called his name softly as she climbed under the covers in the bed and burrowed her way into his side. The king-size memory-foam bed he had was a far cry better than the tiny twin-size beds at the hospital. "Do you . . . Never mind."

"You can't just start off a sentence like that and say never mind," he told her. "I'll go crazy second-guessing what you were going to ask."

Her gaze met his, and he saw ... fear? She wasn't one to be very vulnerable, always keeping a tough exterior. It looked like she was afraid to let that part of her out, and yet ... she did. For him.

"I was going to ask ... do you want to redo our date night in Vegas sometime? Maybe you come out and visit me?"

He quickly nodded. "I'd absolutely love that."

"Good." She beamed and placed a kiss against his chest where her head lay. "I'd really like that, but ... is it too much?"

"Is what too much?" he asked, not understanding the question.

"The long-distance thing." She bit the corner of her bottom lip. "My life is in Vegas, and it's going to be for the foreseeable future. Your life is here ... and kind of everywhere. You travel so much. Can we make something like that work?"

He inhaled deeply, thinking about her question seriously. Long distance was a difficult strain on any relationship, and hell, he'd move to Vegas right now if he thought she wouldn't freak out at the gesture. She didn't seem ... there ... yet. She was skittish and nervous, and he wanted her to fully embrace who they were together first.

"I think that Los Angeles and Vegas are a short flight away from each other, and that if we want something badly enough ... we can make anything work," he finally told her. "So, I guess the question is ... do you want to make this work with me?"

Innocent, big eyes stared up at him. "I do."

His chest clutched at her words, his heart pounding hard against his ribs. "Good. I do too."

He leaned down and kissed her softly on the forehead.

"In the meantime," he began, "we could take advantage of ... tonight."

She lifted her head. "Didn't the doctor say you need to rest?"

"He said a lot of things," Callan said, waving aside the rules like they meant nothing to him. Because ... they really didn't. All that mattered was she was here right now and he wanted to spend more time with her. "That just means that you need to be on top."

Josie laughed and then sat up and turned to straddle her leg across his lap.

"Suit yourself," she replied.

Leaning down, she placed a kiss against his lips. His mouth parted, and she let her tongue explore farther. They danced with each other, teasing as she gave a little and then he gave more. His lip where it was cut stung with each movement, but he pushed aside the pain. He didn't give a shit how hurt he was—nothing was going to stop him from enjoying every inch of Josie's body.

Reaching for the hem of her shirt, he gripped the fabric and pulled it up and over her head, separating them for a moment.

Josie reached behind her and unfastened her bra, letting it fall in a pile between them. He tossed it off the bed and then slid his hands up her stomach to the bottom of her breasts. Cupping them, he held each in his palm and let his thumbs graze over her nipples.

She shuddered, her nipples perking up beneath his touch. Her eyes closed as she let her head fall back slightly. She pumped her hips up and down, even though they were still both fully clothed. His dick jumped to attention, growing harder with every second she writhed on top of him.

"Callan..." she moaned out his name, and it sounded

like sex against her lips.

He slid his hands back down her stomach until he got to the hem of her pants. He pushed them down her hips, and she maneuvered herself to help him get them off her. Next were her panties, which she took off herself, as he shimmied out of the sweatpants he was wearing. Their clothes all got thrown to the floor as she pushed the sheets and blankets out of their way.

"Top drawer in the nightstand," he told her, pointing to the side of the bed.

Josie leaned over and opened the nightstand drawer. Grabbing a foil packet, she pulled it out and ripped it open. He moved to take it from her, but she moved her hands out of reach.

"I want to put it on you," she said, a teasing, sultry tone in her voice.

Callan lifted one brow. "Be my guest."

She positioned the condom at the head of his dick and rolled it down. He jolted at the feeling of her fist around him. The warmth of her hand, the expectation of what was about to happen . . . fuck, he could have come right then and there.

She slid her hips up farther, pushing onto her knees to position herself on top of him. Slowly, tauntingly, she slid down onto his cock.

"Fuck . . ." He groaned at the warm, tight feeling and gripped her hips. He thrust his hips upward and pulled hers down.

She moaned in response, her head falling backward as her tits bounced in his face. Between her pushing up and down on top of him and him thrusting his cock inside her, she rode him hard.

"You feel amazing," she said, her words broken and

pausing between pumps of his dick.

He wanted to make her feel amazing—even more so. Sliding one hand between them, he found her clit and rubbed against it with his thumb.

She bucked forward, her hands falling to his chest as she braced herself against him. Her eyes closed, and a guttural breath escaped her.

The very sound nearly pushed him over the edge, and he sped up his movements, pounding against her as he carefully rubbed her clit. Within moments, he could feel her pulsing around him and she cried out.

He didn't need any more coaxing after that, his own climax hitting him just as hard, as he slammed his hips up against her and emptied himself inside her. He could still feel her contracting around him, pulling every ounce out of him that she could.

When they were both fully spent, she slid off and fell onto the mattress beside him. Tugging the sheet up around her, she curled into his side and sighed contentedly.

"Someone's happy," he teased, wrapping an arm around her shoulders and drawing her even closer to him.

"Mmm." She sighed again and tilted her head up to look at him from where she was resting against his shoulder. "That was amazing."

"Jos," he started, trying to decide what he wanted to say. If he was being honest, he'd tell her that he'd loved the last few days with her. That they felt like a real couple—that she felt like she was his.

That he wanted her to be his.

But he couldn't tell her that.

The woman was a goddamn flight risk, and he had to

tiptoe cautiously or he might lose her entirely.

"Jos," he began again. "I'm going to miss you being here."

She glanced up at him again, sincerity on her expression as her brows pulled together and a small frown played at the corners of her lips.

"I'm going to miss waking up in your arms every morning," she admitted, a slight red blush creeping up her cheeks as he stared at her. "It's been really nice being here . . . being away from everything."

"Are you free this weekend?" he asked her. "I can come to Vegas."

She shook her head. "I work weekend nights, but I'm free next Monday. Mondays and Tuesdays are my days off."

"I'll be there next Monday, then."

"Callan . . ."

He put a finger to her lips. "I'll be there Monday."

Her mouth twitched, the hint of a smile teasing. "Okay," she responded simply. "I'll see you on Monday, then."

The truth was . . . he wasn't sure he could wait.

CHAPTER TWENTY-NINE

"You what?" Samson balked, looking up from his iPhone to stare at Callan.

"I have a girlfriend," Callan repeated, trying not to roll his eyes at his assistant's feigned theatrics.

"Damn, you hit things off with Michelle Rae that well?" Samson asked. "It's supposed to just be a publicity stunt. You know that, right?"

Callan shook his head. "Not Michelle. That's over."

And man, was he glad it was. After all the hell Josie had given him last year about living authentically and not using her for publicity, he couldn't believe he'd been roped into a relationship for the cameras. He couldn't even believe he'd strongly considered giving that a real shot. He'd known immediately it wasn't for him, but he'd stuck with it for almost two weeks . . . and why?

He wasn't sure.

Losing in the championship fight had given him an entirely new perspective on life . . . on everything. Going down like that had awoken a fight in him that he hadn't even known he had. He'd spent the last year—hell, maybe years—living in a play orchestrated by other people. He hadn't been at the wheel of his own life. He went where Samson told him to go. He trained how Ferguson told him to train. He showed up where his schedule dictated he was supposed to be. He left every decision in his life up to his management and team.

Being with Josie again—really *being* with her—was the first decision he'd made for himself in a long time.

And he wasn't letting go.

He'd known the moment he saw her after their year apart that he'd never stopped having feelings for her. And now? They'd only doubled. He was bursting with excitement about being with her, and there was nothing that was going to change his mind.

"Then who?" Samson asked, glancing back down at his phone and scrolling through. "Yeah, I don't have anyone else on your calendar. Who the hell have you been secretly dating?"

"Josie Gray."

Samson's brows shot up. "The reality television star?"

"She hasn't been on television in over a year," Callan clarified.

"Yeah, she's completely fallen off the map until a week ago when she launched her Instagram page again." Samson held up his phone, showing her Instagram feed to him. "She's already gained five hundred thousand new followers since the return. Her cred is going through the roof right now."

Callan hadn't been watching her followers, but he wasn't surprised. People had been upset that she'd disappeared. She was missed, and it made sense that her coming back would cause a big splash.

"This is . . . this is great," Samson said, his face lighting up. Callan could practically see his brain ticking into marketing mode as he went over every way they could exploit this situation. "You all have history, so the paps won't doubt that it's real. You also could get her to agree to go back on the show with her brother—and bring you on as a side character in a few episodes again."

"I'm not doing any of that." Callan said, quickly cutting off his assistant. "This *is* real. And I don't want it to become a public spectacle. I'm only telling you because I'm going to need you not to schedule anything for me on Mondays and Tuesdays from now on. I'll be spending those days in Vegas with her every week."

Samson huffed. "Excuse me?"

"She's not a means to an end, Samson. She's my girlfriend." Callan wanted to make his point very clear. "And you? You're to stay away from her."

"What? Why?" Samson looked as annoyed as Callan felt.

"Because I don't want anyone messing this up for me. I do a good enough job at that myself."

Samson laughed. "Fair enough. But . . . I like this one for you."

Callan just lifted a brow, looking for more of an explanation.

"You've never really put your foot down like this before," Samson continued. "You clearly really like her. Don't let her get away . . . again."

"Thanks, Sam," Callan replied.

"Plus, just think of the press we could get over a wedding between the two of you . . ." Samson had stars in his eyes again.

"Samson . . ." Callan cautioned.

His assistant put his hands up. "Fine, fine. We won't discuss it. Yet."

Callan laughed, shaking his head. "Anyway, can you book me a flight to Vegas on Monday morning with a return on Wednesday morning?"

Samson nodded. "Got it, boss."

"Also, I need to send a bouquet of flowers to Michelle

Rae with an apology note, just thanking her for everything and wishing her well in the future."

"What did you do?" Samson eyed him.

Callan shrugged his shoulders, not wanting to say. "Nothing really, but I definitely hurt her. I want to try to make things right."

"The biggest bouquet they have, then," Samson replied, ticking away at his phone as he began pulling up florist websites. "Anything else?"

"You should book yourself a vacation soon," Callan told him. "You've been working really hard, and I'm taking a step back for the next few months. So take advantage of that."

"You don't have to tell me twice." Samson grinned. "I'll text Elliott right now. I'll need at least a week off."

"Take two," Callan insisted.

After all, Samson did truly work incredibly hard for him. He hadn't had a vacation in over a year. He needed the relaxation as much as Callan needed a break from him and this entire world. He was going to return to his roots ... and his roots intertwined with one person and one person only.

Josie.

CHAPTER THIRTY

"I can't believe you're here," Callan told Josie as he threw his arms around her and lifted her off the ground. He spun her in a circle, her knees bent and her feet up in the air. "I wasn't expecting to see you until later."

"Well, I wasn't going to let you taxi to my apartment by yourself," she said, hugging him back with her arms tight around his neck.

It had only been a week since they'd seen each other, but it felt like forever.

Callan smiled down at her, appreciating the gesture she'd made to come pick him up at the airport. It was insanely early on a Monday morning, and being that this was her day off, he'd expected she would have slept in.

"Come on," she urged, pulling at his arm in the direction of the parking garages. "Let's go have some breakfast."

His stomach growled in response to the thought of food. "I'm starving."

"There's a little diner on the way back to the strip," she told him. "It's in the middle of Murderville and completely abandoned, but the food is phenomenal. It's a little hidden treasure."

"Breakfast in Murderville works for me," he agreed.

Twenty minutes later, they were pulling off the highway next to a rundown mobile home on the side of the highway that had been converted into a diner. It was the size of a double-wide trailer, and the diner's sign had fallen partially off its holder and was crooked. She wasn't kidding—it really did look like a crime scene.

"How did you find this place?" he asked as they walked in through the front door, a bell jingling overhead.

"I desperately had to use the bathroom on my way back from the airport once, so I stopped here." She chuckled at the memory as she retold it. "Everything smelled so good, I decided to have a bite. Never looked back."

Callan's lips twitched, but he hid his smile. "Quite the stroke of luck."

They seated themselves, and in a minute or two, the waitress came over to take their orders. She was in her sixties, at least, but looked closer to eighty years old. Thick makeup coated her face, and she had long, false eyelashes that stuck out much farther than normal.

"I'm Judy, and I'll be your server today. How are you folks doing?" the older woman asked, pulling a pad of paper and a pen out of the pocket of her apron.

"Fantastic, thank you," Callan responded. "I'll have the western omelet, and can you sub the home fries for fresh fruit?"

Josie gave him a bewildered look, one brow higher than the other. "Judy, ignore him. We'll both have an order of silver dollar pancakes—extra butter on top—and a side of crispy bacon and sausage."

Callan laughed and then shrugged his shoulders. "Well, all right, then. Let's do that, Judy."

She nodded, writing down their order and walking away without saying anything.

"Fresh fruit?" Josie balked, lowering her voice. She gave him a teasing grin. "Callan, we're at a diner in a trailer—not the

Bellagio. It's full-fat diet or nothing."

He threw his hands up. "My apologies for trying to be healthy."

"I'll forgive you this time," she said with a laugh.

Callan looked at her for a moment, taking in everything he could about her. Her perfect tight black curls were falling across her face every time she laughed. Bright-green eyes shimmered as she looked at him, and it was everything he could do not to get lost in them. Her lips were perfect and a soft brown that he just wanted to run his tongue across.

"I've really missed you," he finally said, his voice low and sincere.

She tilted her head to the side, a small smile on her lips. "I missed you too."

"I know I've said a lot of things since we've been back in each other's lives, and I'd understand if you found it overwhelming," Callan started, feeling the need to explain himself to her. The urge to tell her how much she meant to him. "But I want you to know that I've meant every word."

"Callan . . ." A soft blush crept up her cheeks.

"I never told you this . . . hell, we never really had the time before, but I don't have any family," he continued.

Her brow furrowed, and she looked sadly at him.

"I'm an only child. My mother died when I was in high school—ovarian cancer—and my father? Well, I never knew who he was. Still don't. That secret died with my mother." Callan sighed. "I never really felt like I had a place I belonged before. A home. So I built my own home and my own family of friends. I tried to build a life that was so grand, so successful, that I wouldn't even have time to think about what I was missing."

"I'm so sorry, Callan," Josie said, reaching out a hand across the table to squeeze his.

He intertwined his fingers with hers. "The reason I'm telling you this, Jos, is that I don't feel that way anymore. It happened instantaneously, to be honest. Last year, when we first met . . . when we first buried a sex doll together . . ."

Josie laughed. "Oh, my God, I forgot about that. Poor Sienna."

Callan smiled, remembering the insanity of that moment. "When all of that happened last year, I felt at home. With you, Jos, I began to realize . . . home isn't a place or something you're born into. It's a person. And for me? It's you."

Tears welled on Josie's bottom lashes, but she batted them away and sniffed. "Callan . . ."

"You don't have to say anything in response," he assured her. "I don't need to know how you feel . . . yet. Take your time. I just want you to know that when I saw you again, after all this time, it hit me. I made a huge mistake letting you walk away last year. I should have chased you. I should have told you we could have made the distance and careers work. I'd make anything work . . . just to be with you. I love you, Jos."

She didn't respond, but she squeezed his hand across the table. "I can't wait for the next two days with you, Callan. And even more . . ."

Leaning forward across the table, he kissed her softly. And this time? He wasn't ever letting go.

CHAPTER THIRTY-ONE

One month later...

"This is enough," Callan said, tossing his shirt with force into his suitcase. "I'm not doing this anymore."

Josie looked up from where she was seated on the bed, reading a book. She truly had no idea what he was referencing. He'd been packing his small suitcase for the drive back to Los Angeles tomorrow morning, when he'd suddenly stopped and started growling, pacing back and forth.

"What?" she asked, hoping for clarification.

"I can't do this anymore," Callan told her. He picked the suitcase up off the bed and placed it down on the floor, zipping it closed. Standing back up, he stared at her with his hands on his hips. "This is now the fourth time I've been to Vegas this month, and we get two days together, and then... that's it. On to the next week."

She swallowed hard, putting down her book. "Callan... what are you saying?"

"I'm saying that I can't keep doing this back and forth," he reiterated. "I'm standing here packing my suitcase for the billionth time this month. Seeing you once a week and then not again for another five days. It's torture."

She scrambled to the edge of the bed to sit next to him as he sat down on the mattress. "I know it's not ideal... but we said we'd make the long-distance thing work."

He shook his head. "I know we said that, but I just can't handle it. I need to be with the person I'm with. I need to see you every day. I need to be able to hug and kiss and everything that comes with being in love."

A lump began to form in her throat as she realized what he could be saying. "Are you . . . are you saying you no longer want to be together?"

Callan whipped his head around to face her, his brows scrunched together and a confused look on his face. "What? No. The opposite. I want us to be together all the time."

"Oh." Well, that answer was a lot better than she had expected. It was also impossible, but she wasn't about to burst his bubble.

"That's why . . . I'm going to start looking at houses in the area," he said. "I'm going to put the place in Los Angeles on the market and move out here."

Her jaw dropped, her mouth falling open.

"That is, if you're okay with it," he clarified. "I want you to be one hundred percent on board and part of the real estate process with me, because . . . well, I'd like you to move in with me."

If her jaw hadn't already been on the floor, it would have been now.

"You want me to what?"

He turned to face her, taking her hands in his. "I want you to move in with me."

Her eyes widened. "Callan, we . . . we just started dating."

"Have we?" he asked. "I know it's technically been a month, but it feels a hell of a lot longer than that. It feels like over a year, because in some ways, it has been."

He had a point there, and she knew it. Hell, it felt like even longer than that. He felt like a part of her life, a part of her.

"I guess it's not that crazy..." she admitted finally, trying to tame the small smile that was creeping up at the corner of her lips. "But what about your work?"

He shrugged his shoulders. "The training center is here. All the major fights are in Vegas. The other ones I would travel to the same as I travel now."

"But what about your reality television career..."

He'd been appearing in the occasional reality television show here and there over the last year—usually on the arm of one of the girls in the show itself. She'd been keeping tabs on him, even though that wasn't part of her career anymore. Sure, it sucked to see him so often with women, but it wasn't until Michelle Rae that he'd actually been spotted in public with any of them. So she'd known it was just an act for the show—something she was quite familiar with from her previous life.

Callan laughed, his face splitting wide into a grin. "This will be the perfect excuse to get the fuck out of that shit."

"Oh, yeah?" she teased, poking his side. "You're not all about the glitz and glamour of Hollywood anymore? If I remember correctly, that's all you wanted from me last year."

He tackled her onto the mattress, pulling them back into the center of the bed. "You know full well that last year had nothing to do with your television career."

She smirked. "What did it have to do with, then?"

He placed a kiss against her neck, licking a short line up to her jaw and kissing her again. "The way you taste. The way you feel beneath me. The way my heart speeds up whenever you're around."

She felt like her heart was melting from his words. "Keep going," she prompted, egging him on.

"Last year had to do with the way you look at me—green eyes sparkling like a forest on fire. Or the way you smile with your whole soul. It's ... it's intoxicating."

"Now you're just being mushy," she replied, pushing him off and pulling away.

He grabbed her and rolled her right back beneath him. Her strength was no match for him, and she laughed at the way he just manhandled her however he wanted.

"I'm being serious, Jos." He made it a point to look in her eyes when he said that, and she felt every inch of his sincerity. "I love you. I loved you last year, and I didn't even know it. But now? There isn't a doubt in my mind. You're the woman for me."

His cell phone pinged, and he glanced over at it. "Ignore that," he told her.

She nodded, but then her cell phone pinged as well. She giggled. "Looks like someone wants our attention."

That seemed to be the truth because both of their phones went off again, and this time, Callan's didn't stop.

"What the hell?" He pushed up off the bed and walked over to the dresser that his phone was sitting on top of. Grabbing it, he looked at the screen.

Josie watched as the color drained from his face.

"What? What's going on?" she asked, panic starting to build in her.

He didn't seem to hear her, because he just kept clicking through his phone.

Josie reached over to the nightstand and grabbed her phone. She opened up her first notification—a Google alert she'd set up to follow Callan's name appearing in the news. She fully admitted it was slightly weird, but hey, it had been a nice way of keeping up with him while they were apart. Now they were together and she couldn't have been happier.

Or at least . . . *had been* happy.

E! NEWS IS FIRST TO REPORT THE IDENTITY
OF MICHELLE RAE'S BABY DADDY.

Josie's hands started shaking as she clicked on the news article and it popped open on her phone.

Surprise! Bikini super model Michelle Rae has announced her first pregnancy in a scathing Instagram post where she points the finger at UFC Championship Fighter Callan Walsh as the father. Walsh and Rae had been seen together several times over the summer, and rumors had been circulating about their potential relationship.

Rae confirmed rumors directly to E! News that not only had she and Walsh been an item for the last few months, but they'd also conceived a child together. Now nine weeks along, Rae claims that her relationship to Walsh ended abruptly after he cheated on her with an unknown woman.

Sources say that the UFC Champion has declined any involvement in his future child's life and is refusing to pay child support. More information to come as this case continues to unfold.

Josie slowly lifted her gaze to Callan. He was staring at her now. His face was white as a sheet, and he looked like he was going to throw up.

"Did you read it?" he asked, barely above a whisper.

She nodded.

"I . . . I didn't know. She never told me." His words came out disjointed and stuttering, like he was just absorbing it himself for the first time. "I'm . . . I'm going to be a father?"

Josie didn't know what to say, but she felt like her heart was breaking. The man she was falling in love with . . . or maybe already loved . . . was having a baby with someone else. And a bikini supermodel, at that. She wanted to scream. She wanted to throw something at him and ask how he could have been so stupid—how he could have even slept with anyone else.

Sure, they hadn't been together. Hell, he'd had no idea she was ever coming back or wanted to be together. It was understandable that after a year apart, he would have moved on to someone else. But then . . . how could he sit here and tell her he loved her? How could he tell her he wanted to spend the rest of his life with her, be only with her, when he'd never mentioned once that things had been this serious with Michelle?

Serious enough to create life.

"Josie, I don't know what to say . . ." He licked his lips, swallowing hard.

"Is it true?" she asked, clenching her jaw. "Were you two . . . together?"

He hung his head, placing his phone in his pocket. "We slept together one time, a month before we started fake-dating for cameras. It was a one-night stand after we met in a club. It's why our public relations teams thought we'd be a good match for the faux relationship for PR purposes."

"Nine weeks ago?" Josie clarified.

Callan shrugged his shoulders slightly. "I didn't really keep track, but . . . that sounds about right."

Josie felt anger bubbling up inside her, threatening to

burst. This was exactly why she'd held back on sharing her feelings with him. She'd felt in her gut that there was more to the story... that it wasn't safe yet. And it turned out her gut was right. He'd been lying to her this entire time.

"You told me there was nothing between you and her. You told me you've loved me since last year. You told me so much shit, and I'm supposed to just, what, ignore the fact that you're about to have a child? With another woman?"

He shook his head. "Jos, I'm so sorry. I don't know how this happened. I have to talk to her."

"And you're refusing to pay child support or even be involved in the kid's life?" Josie asked, ignoring his apology. "How could you do that? Not only are you the world's shittiest boyfriend, but you're going to be a shitty father, too?"

"No!" he almost shouted, and Josie sat back, a little surprised at his outburst. "I had no idea. I didn't even know she was pregnant. If she is... well, I'd never abandon my child. I would—*I will*—take care of any child of mine. You know what my life was like growing up. I'd never, ever do to a child what my father did to me."

Josie paused for a moment, trying to collect her thoughts. None of it made sense. It didn't add up. This wasn't Callan. This article... who it described... it wasn't the man she knew. It wasn't the man she had fallen for... was falling in love with. She felt like such a bitch attacking him in this moment when he must be so conflicted and confused. Her heart ached as she tried to decide what to say, what to do.

"I'm sorry, Callan. I'm sorry this is happening. But... go talk to her," she finally said. "Now."

Callan stayed put for a moment, staring at her, clearly trying to decide what to say. Finally, he just nodded, grabbed his suitcase, turned on his heel, and walked out of the bedroom.

She fell back onto the mattress and didn't bother to wipe away the tears sliding down her cheeks.

After everything they'd gone through... just when everything seemed perfect... it had all come crumbling down around her.

CHAPTER THIRTY-TWO

"Cal?" Samson said on the other end of the line when the call connected. "You there?"

"Here," Callan responded, holding the phone up against his shoulder as he lifted his suitcase and placed it into the trunk of his car. Climbing into the front seat, he turned the phone on speaker and placed it on the dash so he wasn't holding it as he drove. "I need her address, Samson. Text it to me now."

"You can't just go over there," Samson told him. "This is a shit show, Cal. You don't want to make it worse. Clearly, she's mad and has a vendetta against you. We need to tread delicately."

"Give. Me. The. Address," Callan repeated. He wasn't playing around, and he wasn't about to PR this situation to death. He was facing his responsibilities head-on. And his baby? Hell, that was the biggest responsibility of all.

Samson sighed into the other end of the line. "Texting it to you now. But keep me in the loop, Cal. I need to know what's happening if I'm going to fix this for you."

There was nothing to fix. He'd made the mistake, and he was the one who was going to solve his own problems. Clicking off the phone, he pulled open his text messages and plugged in the address that Samson had just texted him.

Putting the car in drive, he headed in the direction of Michelle's home.

Every thought possible crossed his mind as he drove. He

felt like he was going through the five stages of grief on the car ride alone. First, he let anger overtake him. Anger at himself. He'd relied on the pull-out method when he'd been with Michelle—a drunken mistake he'd definitely regretted, but he'd been so sure it had worked. Obviously, he'd been stupid and wrong.

Next, he found himself praying and sending as many positive vibes as he could that this situation would resolve itself somehow—that maybe it was a hoax. Maybe it wasn't true. Maybe it was a stunt for publicity. Denial hit him strong as he tried to reason the situation. This couldn't be happening. It didn't make any sense.

Then the heartache hit, and he felt a lump forming in his throat and tears prickling at the corners of his eyes. He'd always wanted to be a father, sure, but he'd wanted that with one person—Josie. Pain pulsed through his chest as he thought of what this might do to his relationship with her. They'd spent the last month together so happy, so content, so in the groove of what their entire future could be . . . and now he had thrown a piece of dynamite at it all.

But it didn't matter now. He had a child on the way, and if there was one thing he knew for certain, it was that he was going to be a good father. He was going to fight for joint custody. He was going to provide for that child—and for Michelle. He was going to be the father he'd wished he had when he was growing up.

He was going to love his child.

Something he'd never experienced from his father.

Callan took a deep breath and did his best to accept the situation he was in. It wasn't ideal. It wasn't what he'd planned. Hell, it threw all his plans out the window. But . . . it was happening.

And he was going to embrace it.

Children were a gift, and this ... he was going to see this as a gift.

A few hours later, he arrived at Michelle's house in Los Angeles. It was a small ranch-style home overlooking the beach. The view was beautiful and the house even more beautiful. It was clear that she'd done well with her career to afford a location like this, and he felt grateful that his future child would live in a home like this.

"What are you doing here?" Michelle's eyes grew wide as she opened the front door after he'd knocked on it.

"Is it true?" he asked. "Well, I know parts of it aren't true— but the baby? Are you pregnant? Is it mine?"

Her hands immediately went to her stomach, as if protectively covering herself. Sure enough, he could see the smallest swell across her abdomen that had never been there before. Michelle had always had a flat stomach with abs to die for. There was no doubt that she was definitely pregnant now.

"Do you think I'd lie about a baby?" she shot back. "Seriously, Cal?"

"I'm sorry," he said, shaking his head. "But you can imagine how shocked I was to hear what a shitty father I was on *E! News*—when I didn't even know I was a father."

Her gaze dropped for a moment, and then she lifted it back to his. "Look, I'm sorry for how you found out. That wasn't my idea. My manager thought it would create good buzz for the show coming up. We actually want you to be on it."

"My reality television days are over," Callan told her. "But if that's my baby, I'm not going anywhere."

"So ... you're what? Going to marry me? Make me an honest woman?" She tilted her head to the side and held up her left hand, wiggling her fingers. "Because I don't see a ring on this finger."

Callan balked at the thought. It was one thing to have a baby with a woman who wasn't Josie, but he for sure wasn't about to marry someone else. As much as he wanted his future child to have a healthy and stable home, that wasn't going to be with two parents who didn't love each other.

"I ... I'm sorry, Michelle," he replied. "I can't do that. But I can, and will, be here to take care of my child. Your article said that I had declined to be part of the child's life, and that couldn't be further from the truth."

She lifted her chin slightly, clearly miffed at the conversation. "Well ... good. I'll need the help. Being a single mom wasn't exactly on my bucket list. But I can't really stick around and have it out with you right now. I have a doctor appointment to get to."

"Can I come with you?" he asked, eager for the chance to see how his baby was doing.

She looked tentative for a moment, as if trying to decide what she wanted to do. Finally, she nodded her head. "Okay. But ... you're paying."

"Happily," he replied. "Come on. I'll drive us."

Fifteen minutes later, they were pulling up to a large office building.

"Is this Daddy?" the nurse asked with a bright smile as they were called from the waiting room into the back.

Michelle beamed and wrapped an arm around his shoulders. "It is."

"Well, congratulations, Daddy," the nurse responded, leading them to an examination room.

"Thanks." Callan stood next to the exam table as Michelle

climbed on and leaned back. "You okay?"

Michelle nodded. "I feel fine. A little nauseated, but that's about it."

They fell into an awkward silence as they waited for the doctor. Neither one of them said anything, though Callan tried to think of a topic. He came up blank. Thankfully, the doctor came in minutes later and relieved them of their silence.

"How are we doing today, Ms. Rae?" the doctor asked, setting up the necessary equipment.

"Fine." She glanced up at Callan. "This is the father."

"Welcome, Daddy," the doctor greeted him. "Nice to have you join us. We're going to check the heartbeat today and make sure everything is going well."

The doctor squirted gel onto Michelle's stomach and then placed a monitor against her skin, moving it around as she watched the corresponding screen. Within a few moments, a loud, fast galloping sound filled the room.

Callan's eyes widened, and his heart began to race as he realized what he was hearing.

"There's the heartbeat," the doctor announced. "Strong. Fantastic."

He was listening to his baby's heartbeat. A real, living, tiny being, right there in her stomach who was half him. Sure, he'd known for the last few hours that she'd been pregnant with his child, but there was something entirely different about actually seeing the proof in front of him. The heartbeat pounded around them, and it *was* strong and fast. Callan couldn't keep the smile from widening across his face as he listened to his future son or daughter.

"Wow," he said.

Michelle reached for him, and he let her take his hand.

She gave him a squeeze, and he returned it. "That's our baby, Cal."

He just nodded his head, staring at the screen with the small image of their future baby. He couldn't find the words, couldn't speak. He couldn't say or do anything but stare at the little miracle in front of him.

As much as he'd felt earlier like this situation had been a disaster that was ruining his relationship and his future, he couldn't be further away from that thought now. He was going to be a father. He was going to have a baby.

And sure, it wasn't the ideal circumstances, and it wasn't with the woman he loved, but . . . it was his baby. He was already in love with the tiny being, and they'd never even met. It didn't matter. His heart was bursting at the seams. He saw his whole life unfolding in front of him—Christmases around the tree with the baby on his knee, teaching him or her how to ride a bike for the first time, taking pictures and embarrassing the shit out of his child on prom night, when going on the first date.

Actually, scratch that. His child wouldn't be allowed to date. Not until age thirty. Maybe forty.

He pictured dancing with his future daughter at her wedding or tying his future son's bowtie before he got married. He pictured summers on a lake with his grandchildren and even more babies all around him.

"You're smiling," Michelle said, nodding toward him.

"I can't help it," he admitted, and then he paused for a moment. "Michelle . . . thank you. Thank you for this. Our baby . . . it's a gift. A blessing."

A pink blush lifted onto her cheeks as she cleaned the gel off her stomach after the doctor was done. "Well . . . I couldn't have done it without you."

Callan laughed, and any anger he might have felt toward Michelle and her public attack on him was gone. This was the mother of his expected child, and damn it, he was going to make nice. He was going to be the rock she could lean on—for their child's sake.

The doctor left them alone in the room for a few minutes as Michelle finished cleaning herself up.

"I'm not going anywhere," Callan told her. "I want to be involved in this baby's life. I want to help you raise our child. I will pay child support, do joint custody. Anything. I'll be here for you every day, Michelle."

She looked up at him, searching his eyes as if she didn't quite believe what he was saying. "Okay," she replied simply. "I guess . . . I guess we're doing this."

He nodded, thinking about everything he might lose because of this decision.

CHAPTER THIRTY-THREE

"Order up!" Josie slid the plate full of food under the heating rack, grabbed the next order from the ticket machine, and stuck it up on the board in front of her.

It had been four days since she'd last seen or spoken to Callan. Josie had busied herself with work, picking up extra shifts and keeping her phone off as much as possible. She didn't want to talk to him. She didn't want to hear about how he was moving on with his new family.

One she wasn't a part of.

She didn't want to have her heart broken more than it already was. And it truly was. With every minute he was gone, Josie realized more and more just how much he had meant to her. She regretted every second she'd held back. Why hadn't she told him that she loved him, too? That she wanted to spend the rest of her life with him?

Because that was the truth. The longer they were apart, the more that had become evident. She wouldn't be this forlorn, this hurt, if she didn't have real feelings involved.

She loved him. It was that simple.

"Gray, did you hear me?" Rockport called from the other side of the kitchen.

She quickly snapped her head up. "Oh. Sorry. Say that one more time?"

"I said your shift is over. Clock out. You've been here twelve hours straight." Rockport looked down at his watch and shook his head. "I'm not about to have my new star chef burn out."

She washed her hands off and began unbuttoning her chef's jacket. "Yes, sir."

Clocking out back in the office, Josie went about gathering her things. Turning on her cell phone for the first time all day, she wasn't surprised when it buzzed a few dozen times with new messages and notifications. The first text message to pop up was from Callan.

Can we talk?

She paused. He'd been silent for days, but suddenly he was texting her that they needed to talk? Her stomach dropped as she realized this was probably his way of meeting to break up with her.

Not answering yet, she opened up her Instagram app on her phone. Even though she knew it was torture, she couldn't help but to go to Michelle Rae's feed to see if she'd posted anything new. Sure enough, once she clicked through, she found a picture of Michelle and Callan in what looked like a doctor's office. Michelle's shirt was pushed up and a doctor was performing an ultrasound on her stomach. Both Callan and Michelle were radiating smiles and looked over the moon for their little bundle of joy.

If she hadn't already been worried that Callan was going to dump her, this photo confirmed it. He was moving on with his new family. He was happy with them—with her.

Josie was an afterthought at best. A slice of his past.

Returning to her text messages, she responded to him.

Sure.

He wrote back quickly.

Tonight. O'Hannigans?

She agreed and then stuck her phone in her pocket, ready to head home and take a long nap before heading out to get dumped at her favorite bar.

A few hours later, Josie was finished preparing for the evening. She'd picked out one of her favorite cocktail dresses— not too fancy so as to stand out at the dive bar, but just stylish enough to look like she didn't give a damn about any man. Her makeup was done perfectly, and her hair was set just the right way to make it look effortless.

Walking into O'Hannigans, she glanced around the room to spot Callan. Not seeing him, she decided to take a seat at the bar.

"One vodka on the rocks with lime, please," Josie asked the bartender.

He made it for her quickly, returning a glass to her. She took a sip as she looked around the room again.

The front door to the establishment opened, and in walked the man she'd been waiting for. He had one hand in his suit pants pocket, and the other was fastening the buttons of his suit jacket. He looked like he'd just come from a professional event of some kind, and she couldn't help but wonder if he had dressed up for her as well.

"Callan," she called out to him, waving her hand.

He spotted her and came over, taking the stool next to hers at the bar.

"Nice to see you," he said before ordering a drink from the bartender. "I'm sorry I've been MIA for the last few days."

She shrugged. "It looks like you have a lot on your plate."

"You could say that." He chuckled wryly, though nothing about it seemed sincere.

"Callan…" She glanced down at her drink, stirring the small beverage straw with her fingers. "What are we doing here?"

She wanted to rip off the Band-Aid. If he was going to break up with her, he should just do it. She couldn't stand sitting here another minute thinking… what if?

He didn't respond right away. It looked like he was collecting his words, trying to find the most delicate way to let her down. Finally, he spoke.

"Remember how we talked about me moving to Las Vegas? Moving in together? Settling down?"

She nodded.

He looked down again, this time fidgeting with the corner of the bar. "Michelle's in Los Angeles. Our… our baby will be in Los Angeles."

"You can't leave," Josie finished for him.

He shook his head slowly. "No. I can't leave."

"And I just started my job here at Niro's," she added. "So… I can't leave Vegas."

"You shouldn't," he quickly added. "Not when you have such an amazing opportunity here for you."

They were both quiet for a moment. It wasn't an awkward silence, but rather… sad. Sorrow hung between them as they both realized what they were deciding.

"Why does this feel so familiar?" Josie asked, barely above a whisper.

Callan sighed, letting out a deep breath. "Because we did the same thing last year."

He wasn't wrong. Last year, they'd both chosen their careers over having an "*us*." This year, she was choosing her career and he was choosing his future family.

"Timing has never been our strong suit, has it?" He chuckled again, but it sounded even more insincere than last time. It sounded strained... sad.

"And so... here we are." Josie looked up at him, really taking in his eyes and absorbing the emotions he was sharing in that moment. "Separating again."

"We could try long distance..." he offered, obviously trying to hold on to any lifeline.

She didn't want that. She knew he didn't either. He needed to focus on his new son or daughter, not traveling to Vegas every week or even every other week if they switched off. He needed to be there for the pregnancy and the birth.

He needed to be a father right now, not a boyfriend.

"You know we can't," she replied. "You need to be there for Michelle."

He hung his head, a look of guilt crossing his face. "I know."

"One last drink?" she asked him, lifting her finger to the bartender to signal she wanted a second.

"Sure," he agreed, doing the same.

Leaning toward her, he ran his hand up her leg and squeezed her knee. "I'm going to miss you, Jos."

A lump began to form in her throat. She could feel tears pricking at her eyes, but she pushed them away.

"You know what? Cancel that drink," Josie told the bartender, placing a few bills down on the counter.

"What?" Callan looked confused.

Josie stood from her stool and grabbed her purse. "I have to be up early in the morning," she said, not looking him straight in the eyes.

"Jos, don't do this."

It was too late. She was shutting down. She was closing off every open, vulnerable side of herself because it was just too much. It hurt too much—he was hurting her too much. And so, she shut down entirely.

"Don't run off like this," he repeated, taking her hand and trying to pull her in closer to him.

She stepped back and shook her head. "It was nice seeing you, Callan. I hope everything goes well for you. You deserve it."

"Jos—"

"Goodbye," she said, cutting him off. With that, she left the bar as quickly as her legs could carry her without actually sprinting.

The moment she got outside, the tears began to flow down her cheeks. Loud, heaving sobs racked through her as she fumbled with her phone and tried to call a Lyft to pick her up. Finally, she managed to secure one and slumped onto the curb while she waited.

Even though she'd predicted that this was how tonight was going to end, she hadn't been ready for it. It was one thing to know it was coming, but it was another to get slammed across the face with the reality of it all.

"Jos, let me give you a ride." Callan approached her from behind, catching her off guard.

She quickly wiped at the tears on her face and tried to sniff it back. "I'm fine, Callan."

"You're not fine. You're crying."

Josie cut her eyes to him. "You're so observant."

"Is this how you want to end things? You lashing out at me with sarcasm?" Callan folded his arms across his chest, looking exasperated and conflicted all at once. "I don't want to remember us like this, Jos."

She paused for a moment, considering his words. He was right. She didn't want to end things so coldly . . . so hostile. And yet, she couldn't seem to shake the defenses that were climbing their way up between them and stopping any chance he had of getting through to her.

Thankfully, her ride pulled up right then, and Josie stood and opened the passenger-side back door.

"Jos," Callan called after her quietly, his voice full of anguish.

"I'll see you around," she responded, giving him a small wave. "Take care of yourself."

He stood stoically still, watching her get into the car and close the door. The car drove off, leaving a piece of herself shredded on the curb.

CHAPTER THIRTY-FOUR

Five months later...

"You don't think the three different camera crews are a little excessive?" Callan leaned in close to Michelle and whispered in her ear. "It's a baby shower. Not a circus."

She cut her eyes to him and shook her head. She ran a hand over her large, protruding baby bump. "We're filming for the new show. The baby shower is going to be its own episode. Plus, *People* magazine is doing an early exclusive for us."

He furrowed his brow as he looked around the expansive backyard of his Los Angeles home that had been turned into a full-scale party site. Guests were due to arrive any minute, and they'd be hosting a giant combined baby shower and gender-reveal party. "So what's the third camera crew for, then?"

"Personal pictures and video. Don't you want our future child to be able to look back and see what his or her own baby shower was like?" Michelle said it like it was obvious, but there was a hint of guilt-tripping in there as well.

Callan wasn't sure that made an entire film crew necessary, and he'd been against throwing a giant affair like this. But the mother of his child had insisted that this was what she wanted, and he didn't want to say no. In fact, he hadn't said no to any ridiculous request from Michelle in the last five months. While their relationship remained platonic—not for lack of trying on her part—he still bent over backward to accommodate her every whim and wish.

Why? He wasn't entirely sure. He told himself he was doing it because he wanted to be a good father, but . . . was this the way to do it? Every night he went home alone and lay in bed, thinking about his choices. Thinking about the woman he'd left behind to become a father.

Admittedly, he spent more time than he should checking Josie's Instagram page and following what she was up to. She looked . . . well, she looked happy. She often posted pictures of the food she was cooking, photos of her in the kitchen with her chef's coat on, or pictures of places she traveled to on her days off. She seemed to make it a point to take trips almost every week—never staying in Vegas longer than she needed to for work.

"Callan, are you listening to me?" Michelle interrupted, pulling him back to the party.

"What? Sorry." He returned his attention to his future baby mama.

Michelle flared her nostrils in annoyance. "I was saying that someone needs to tell the valets where to park the cars."

He nodded. "I'll do it."

Heading inside the house, he walked through and out the front door to the valet station, where attendants were waiting to park guests' cars. He spent a few minutes showing them where to park and instructed them on what they needed. By the time he was done, guests were already starting to arrive.

"Walsh!" Michael Rockport stepped out of his car—a black Range Rover—and handed his keys to the attendant while calling out to Callan.

Callan waved a hand at his old friend. "Hey, Michael."

"How have you been?" Rockport asked him as they

walked back into the house together. "It's been a few months since I've seen you."

"Well, I'm having a baby," he kidded, as if Rockport didn't already know that.

Rockport smacked him playfully on the back of his shoulder. "Congratulations, man. That's amazing. My three kids are the joy of my life. I don't even know what I did before them."

Callan smiled, thinking of holding his future kid in just a few short weeks. "I can't wait, man."

"Where's your lovely lady? How's she feeling this far into the pregnancy?" Rockport asked.

"She's been doing surprisingly well. A little tired, but that's about it," Callan said. "But, she's actually not *my* lady. We're not together like that. We're just co-parenting."

Rockport lifted his chin, nodding his head slightly. "Ah. I was wondering what was going on there after the Gray situation."

Callan was quiet for a moment as they stood out on the porch while a waiter delivered cocktails. "How is she?" he finally asked.

"Gray?" Rockport replied. "She's amazing. I've expanded her job to head chef, and she's going to be taking over a second restaurant next week."

He lifted his brows. "Really?"

"There's even talk of a cooking show. Her previous producers from the reality show with her brother want to bring her back into the limelight again, but she won't do anything unless it involves cooking."

"And you have your own cooking show," Callan pointed out.

"And my own production company," Rockport reminded him. "Adding a female-driven cooking show to my portfolio might be just what I need."

"You should do it," Callan encouraged his friend. "She's talented. She's charismatic. She'd be amazing at it."

"If she agrees. She's been putting up a hard line about not wanting to get back into show business."

Callan didn't doubt that, not after her previous experiences with the reality television world.

"Her career is definitely blowing up," Rockport continued. "It's her time to shine, and she's breaking into new markets, but... between you and me? I liked you and her a lot better than I like her new beau."

"She's dating someone?" His stomach turned at the thought. He hadn't seen any indication of her dating anyone on her Instagram page.

Rockport nodded and then took a sip of his cocktail. "Well, it's not like she opens up to me about her love life or anything," he clarified. "But this skinny guy has been coming by pretty regularly. He's very loud. And he always sends back his steak and asks for it to be well done. Who does that to steak?"

Callan's eyes widened as he started putting some pieces together. "Excuse me for a minute," he told Rockport as he hurried off.

After doing a few laps around the crowd that had already begun filling up the big tent they'd rented and doing his obligatory hellos to everyone, he spotted his target.

"Samson!" Callan called out, gesturing for his assistant to follow him.

Samson waved back and crossed the tent, coming to join him. They walked back toward the house, out of earshot from the rest of the party.

"What's up, boss?"

"What the actual fuck?" Callan started, turning on his heels and staring down his assistant. "What do you think you're doing?"

The young man threw his hands up in defense. "Whoa, cowboy. Let's slow down for a second and catch me up. What are you talking about?"

"You've been seeing Josie behind my back?" Callan clarified, his jaw clenched as he spoke.

Samson gave him an awkward grin, looking sheepish and guilty as fuck. "Okay, well, to be fair . . . I didn't know you knew about that."

"Samson!"

"What? She's really cool," Samson said. "We've become good friends. You were an idiot for leaving her."

"I can't believe you've been secretly running around town with my ex without telling me." Callan practically growled out his words. "What happened to loyalty? You're *my* assistant."

"Sure, but I'm Elliott's husband, and he has had a girl crush on her for at least five years. So, when I found out you had the connect, I introduced myself. And now? Well, we're good friends. She's a really great person."

"I *know* she's a really great person. I'm the one who's in love with her."

Samson's brows lifted. "In love . . . as in currently?"

Callan paused for a moment, trying to absorb what he'd just said in the heat of the moment and reflect on how he really felt. It had been almost two years since he'd first met Josie and developed feelings for her. If he was being honest with himself, they hadn't lessened any in that time. In fact, they'd only grown stronger.

"I—I don't know," Callan clarified.

"You'd better find out," Samson said. "Because my girl is still holding a torch for you too."

"She is? How do you know that?"

"Girl talk is a mandatory part of being the gay best friend." Samson shrugged his shoulders like it was obvious. "But you have a limited window."

Callan frowned. "What do you mean?"

"I mean, she finally said yes to a date with someone else."

He felt his stomach dropping. "And you didn't stop her?"

Samson squinted his eyes at him. "Are you kidding? I'm the one who set it up. She deserves to be happy. In case you've forgotten, you left her to have a baby with someone else."

He hadn't forgotten. Hell, it was all he could think about some days.

Not responding, he let out a deep sigh and shook his head.

"It'll be fine, Cal," Samson assured him. "You did what you had to do."

"Did I?" Callan asked quietly.

His assistant just gave him a sad look. Callan didn't want to see it anymore, so he walked away and rejoined the party, a fake smile plastered on his face.

CHAPTER THIRTY-FIVE

UFC championship fighter and bikini supermodel Michelle Rae
announce the gender of their future child—it's a girl!

Josie put her phone down and sighed. A daughter. Callan was having a daughter with his baby mama. Were they together? She wasn't sure, but they certainly looked cozy in all the photos online from their gender-reveal party and baby shower.

"What?" Marcus glanced over from where he was seated at the conference table next to her while they waited for the rest of the meeting participants to show up.

She placed her phone facedown on the table. "Nothing."

"Tell me you're not stalking Walsh again," Marcus warned, rolling his eyes.

She felt her cheeks heating. "No," she lied.

"Jos, seriously? You're just torturing yourself."

"I know, okay? Let's just focus on why we're here."

Marcus nodded and looked toward the conference room entrance. "They're running late. It's a fucking power move. You're lucky I'm here instead of Ma, or she'd be out there trying to track them down."

Her new manager, Marcus, was already excelling at the job in the short time since she'd brought him on board. Plus, her stress was significantly lowered not having to work directly with her mother. She loved her mother, but the two often butted heads on what they saw as Josie's future.

"Hey, folks." Jamie Sessions walked in with several older men in suits. "Sorry we're a little late. Can we get you anything to drink?"

Josie shook her head. "No, thank you."

Jamie introduced the other executives he was with, but as soon as he said their names, Josie promptly forgot them. It was just a room of stuffy white men who had control over her future. No big deal.

"So, let's get started on why we're here—Josie's Kitchen." Sessions passed around a stack of papers to everyone in the room. "We've got the first few episodes outlined. We're expecting twenty-two episodes a season—thirty minutes each. Food Network has already agreed to give us the nine o'clock morning slot with potential for replays in the evening if ratings flourish."

Josie raised her brows. "Wow."

"We'll be launching the premiere episode with a red-carpet event, a huge push on Instagram and Twitter, and we'll be bringing celebrity guests on each episode to be your sous chef."

"It looks like you have everything arranged," Josie mused, lifting the papers in front of her and scanning through them. She paused when she got to the location section. "Wait a second... Burbank?"

"We'll be filming in Burbank, five days a week," Sessions confirmed.

"How will I keep working at Niro's?" she asked, confused. She'd been told that doing this show wouldn't disturb her current life and career.

"Uh, yeah... you'll need to move to the Burbank area. We

have a realtor set up and ready to work with you. She's great and more than capable of finding you the perfect home."

"But I live in Las Vegas. Why can't we film here?"

"A number of reasons—lack of a studio, taxes, cast, et cetera."

Marcus put a hand on hers. "We understand, but we're going to need to think about it."

Jamie looked startled. "Think about it?"

"Unless you're willing to sweeten the pot," Marcus countered.

The producer nodded, like he suddenly understood the power play he was currently involved in with her manager. "Moving expenses and down payment on house—covered."

"That's a start," Marcus replied, this time leaning back.

Jamie looked at his business associates, who just gave him a small nod. "We can bump up the salary by ten percent."

"Twenty-five and we'll be closer to considering," Marcus responded. "You pay your male television chefs that amount. Josie should be making the same thing."

The producer inhaled deeply, looking frustrated but also a bit guilty. "We can do fifteen, but that's as high as we go."

"Come on, Josie." Marcus turned to her and stood up from his chair, offering her a hand. "We've got another appointment to get to."

Josie glanced up at him, standing awkwardly. She wasn't really sure what was going on. Negotiations like this were not her strong suit. Plus, she wasn't even sure she wanted the job. After all, did she want to leave Vegas?

"Okay, wait. Twenty-five," Jamie caved. "We can do the twenty-five."

"And executive producer credits in her name," Marcus

added, going for the jugular.

"Sure," Jamie agreed, sighing as his lips were in a tight line. "We can make that work. I'll have the contract redrawn and sent to you this week."

Marcus reached out a hand to Jamie. "Pleasure doing business with you."

Jamie shook Marcus's hand but didn't look nearly as happy as he did. Jamie shook her hand next. "It was nice to see you again, Josie."

"You as well," she replied and then followed her brother out of the conference room.

The moment they got outside the building and out of earshot of anyone who mattered, Marcus turned to her. "We did it!"

Josie grinned. "You did it. That was amazing, Marcus. You were meant to do this."

"Thanks." Marcus beamed as they walked to the car. "It was a rush. So now all we have to do is sign the papers when they come in, and you're good to go for the next chapter of your life."

She was quiet for a moment, and that seemed to give her away.

Her brother eyed her suspiciously. "Jos? Are you okay?"

"I just...I didn't really think I'd have to move out of Vegas," she replied, slightly forlorn at the idea.

Marcus shrugged his shoulders. "Most filming is in California, sis. I'll move out there with you. You won't be alone."

"You will?" That did make her feel slightly better. The idea of being all alone on the West Coast was certainly not her ideal. But...she also couldn't help but think about who she'd be closer to.

Los Angeles and Burbank were practically neighbors.

Did she really want to watch the man she'd fallen in love with raising another woman's baby right in front of her when she couldn't be with him? It sounded like torture.

Then again . . . this was an amazing business opportunity. And it wasn't like she was going to run into him. They didn't exactly run in the same circles. Although, she did recently strike up an amazing friendship with Callan's assistant. They'd started chatting when she and Callan had been together and never let the breakup stop them from remaining friends.

"It won't be so bad, sis," Marcus assured her. "Plus, it's only a four-hour drive back to Vegas to see the family. Hell, the distance between you and Ma is probably a good thing."

Josie chuckled lightly. He wasn't wrong. "You know, Callan lives in Los Angeles," she admitted to her brother.

Marcus lifted one brow as he stared at her over the roof of the car before they both climbed into it. "Walsh? You're not going to run into him. I promise as your manager that I'm going to keep him as far away from you as possible."

"Why?" she asked, curious about her brother's sudden passion for the topic.

Marcus put the car into reverse and backed out of the parking space they were in after they'd both buckled their seat belts. "That asshole left you to get another chick pregnant."

"It's not his fault. They were together before he and I were." Josie suddenly felt the need to defend him. "We weren't together when that happened. He's doing the right thing by being there for his child."

"Sure," Marcus agreed. "He'd be a royal prick if he didn't step up and take responsibility for what he did. But why were you two apart in the first place?"

Josie sighed. "Admittedly . . . that's kind of on me. I left to go to cooking school."

"And what? Phones don't exist?"

Her brother had a point, but at the same time, she was the one who had been holding back the last few times they'd been together. Hell, before he'd found out about his impending fatherhood, Callan had made his intentions very clear to her. He'd told her he loved her—that he wanted to be with her for the rest of his life.

And she'd said nothing back to him.

She'd kept her feelings bottled up and hadn't shared them with him.

Why?

Now she wasn't so sure.

"I think I messed up, Marcus." Her voice was low and strained, a lump starting to form in her throat as she replayed their last breakup in her mind.

He glanced sideways at her. "You really still have feelings for him? After all this time?"

Josie just nodded, staring out the window and watching the street pass her by.

"Well, that's saying something, Jos." Marcus reached over and patted her knee. "Maybe you should do something about that. Maybe you should talk to him."

"Weren't you just the one who called him an asshole?" Josie eyed her brother.

Marcus nodded. "I did, but I see it this way. You either need closure to move on and be happy in life . . . or he's your happiness in life, he's your person. Either way, it's going to involve a conversation with him."

She didn't know when her little brother had become so

wise and knowledgeable, but she was impressed, nevertheless.

"I need a plan," she said, her brain already going into overdrive. She was going to come clean about her feelings for him. She was going to lay it all on the line and hope...pray... that he didn't leave her shattered.

CHAPTER THIRTY-SIX

"Don't forget the nipple cream!" Michelle called out behind him as he walked toward the front door. "We're going to need that once the baby comes."

She was days away from giving birth, and her stomach was basically the size of a beach ball.

Callan nodded his head. "I won't forget. I'll be back with that tomorrow. Call me if anything happens in the meantime."

"Tomorrow?" Michelle waddled into the main foyer of her house, following him. "What about tonight?"

"I've got meetings in the morning," he reminded her. "I need to get a good night's sleep."

Staying up and rubbing her feet while she watched *The Real Housewives of Orange County* had been cutting into his sleep. He didn't mind because he'd do anything to make her feel comfortable, but he was realizing that he needed to start setting some boundaries.

"What if I go into labor tonight?" Michelle continued, placing both hands on her hips. "You're going to miss your own child's delivery?"

"Michelle, I live five minutes away. My house is actually on the way to the hospital from here."

She tilted her head to the side. "If you're closer, then maybe I should stay at your house until the baby comes."

Callan put his hand up between them. "Michelle, no. We're not a couple. We're not dating. You're going to have to get used to being on your own sometime. I'm not going to be living here with you. We're splitting custody—remember?"

Her chin jutted out, and she sized him up as her nostrils flared. "So, you're just going to leave me to raise this baby on my own?"

"You know that's not what I said. I'm going now. I'll talk to you tomorrow. Call me if anything happens before then." Callan headed for the door and walked out. He wasn't about to start an irrational argument with a pregnant woman. He wasn't going to cause her stress.

His phone began ringing in his pocket as he climbed into his car. He pulled it out and answered it while he was buckling his seat belt. "Hello?"

"Hey, Cal." Samson's voice rang through the other end of the line. "Do you have anywhere to be right now?"

"Uh, aren't you my assistant? Shouldn't you be telling me?" Callan said with a laugh as he placed the phone on the dashboard and pulled the car out onto the main road.

"That's my way of saying I know your afternoon is clear and I need you to do something for me."

Samson didn't ask for a lot of favors, so Callan was pretty open to helping his friend when needed.

"Sure, bud. What's up?"

"I'm going to text you an address. Can you meet me there? I'll explain everything when you get there."

Callan furrowed his brow. "I mean . . . I guess I can. What's going on? Why the mystery?"

"It's good. I promise. Just head there now." Samson's voice pulled away for a minute, and then Callan's phone pinged with a new text message. "I just sent you the address. Bye!"

Samson hung up, and Callan stared at his phone, trying to

figure out what the hell his assistant was up to. He placed the address into his GPS. He didn't recognize it, but it was only about a twenty-minute drive. Turning up the radio, he settled in.

He couldn't help but let his mind wander as he drove. There was a listlessness to his life recently. He was about to have a baby—it should be a joyous time in his life. And without a doubt, he was thrilled to become a father soon. He already loved his future daughter more than he could describe. His heart felt like it was going to explode in his chest every time he thought about holding her.

But there was a part of him that still felt . . . empty.

There seemed to be this fog over him that he just couldn't shake, no matter what he did. Being around Michelle made it worse. She kept trying to paint them as this perfect little nuclear family, and he kept having to keep her at arm's length. As much as he wanted a happy family for his future daughter, it couldn't be with someone he didn't love. He wasn't going to model a loveless marriage or relationship for his daughter. No, he wanted her to see fire and passion and unconditional love at its best.

His mind drifted back to the one time he'd ever felt that in his life. At the next red light, he pulled open Josie's Instagram page and scanned through her photos. She still looked as beautiful as he remembered, and she looked incredibly happy in every shot. Her most recent photo was of her lying on a pile of cardboard boxes. The caption read *new beginnings #mood*.

He wondered what that meant. He wanted to reach out to her and text her, ask her what was new with her, but he didn't. It seemed too intrusive. After all, their separation was his fault. He'd hoped they could have stayed friends, but . . . it just seemed too hard. Talking to her felt painful—a reminder of what he'd lost.

Returning his phone to the dashboard, he drove to see Samson. Strangely enough, his assistant was meeting him in a residential neighborhood just outside of Burbank. Callan wondered if Samson was looking at houses, because sure, he paid him well, but he wasn't sure he paid him enough to live in this type of neighborhood.

Pulling up to the address, he looked at a large navy-blue house with white shutters. It wasn't the largest house in the neighborhood, but it was still impressively sized. The front yard was covered in grass and intricate landscaping. It was absolutely beautiful, and sure enough, there was a sign on the front lot that read *Sold*.

Samson had bought himself a house.

Callan climbed out of the car and walked up to the front door. He rang the bell and then waited, taking a step back.

The door swung open after a moment, and a woman stepped into view.

Not just any woman—Josie. His Josie.

"Hi," she greeted him shyly, looking up at him from under long black lashes.

"Jos?" He was completely confused. "Is...is Samson here? I was meeting him."

She shook her head. "He told you to come here for me. He's not here."

"Oh." Callan pushed his hands into his pockets, unsure where to go from here or what to say.

"Do you want to come in?" She gestured toward the inside of the house.

He nodded and stepped over the threshold into the foyer.

"Whose house is this?" he asked, looking around at the cozy and warm interior. "It's really nice."

"Thank you," she responded. "Um . . . it's actually mine. I just bought it."

He swirled around to look at her. "You live here now?"

She bit the corner of her lip. "I do."

Excitement flooded him. He wanted to throw his arms around her and swing her around, begging her to be with him. He wanted to get rid of everything that had happened in the last two years and just be themselves again. Just be who they'd been when they'd first met.

But he said nothing. He'd been down that road before. He'd tried to push her into a relationship, and she'd never budged. She'd kept her feelings locked down tighter than Fort Knox, and he knew better than to try to infiltrate her walls again.

"Welcome to the neighborhood," he simply replied.

She stared at him for a moment and then gave him a small smile. "Thank you."

"What am I doing here, Jos?" he finally asked, curiosity getting the better of him.

"I wanted to show you something," she replied. "Come with me."

He followed her up the stairs and down a hallway to a wing of bedrooms. There were still boxes everywhere, and it was clear that she was still in the process of unpacking everything. He didn't blame her one bit, but it made for some maneuvering as they worked their way around the stacks everywhere.

Finally, she opened a door to her left and motioned for him to go inside. Furrowing his brow, he walked past her and into the room. He immediately stopped in his steps and took in everything he was seeing. The walls had been painted a soft pink—different from the rest of the house, which was traditionally white. There was a crib against the back wall, and a fabric rocking chair in the corner. In fact, it had everything one would need for a baby. The room was move-in-ready for a little girl.

Callan's heart started to race. Was Josie pregnant? Was it his? She hadn't looked pregnant when they met at the door. Turning around, he looked at her.

Except, she wasn't where she'd been standing a moment ago.

She was down on one knee on the floor holding up a small, velvet box with a wedding band inside.

"Josie?" he asked, confused as to what she was doing. "What is this? What is this room?"

"Callan, I have spent the last two years trying to find myself. Trying to figure out who I was outside of the cameras and in my career. I thought that was what would make me happy. I thought I needed to be this independent career woman to complete my life, to finally grow up and get out from under my family's thumb," she explained, still down on one knee in front of him. "But the truth is, now that I have all those things ... and more, I still feel like I'm missing something. Or someone."

He wanted to wrap his arms around her and tell her everything would be okay. "Josie ..."

"The truth is, I've only felt whole twice before ... and both of those times were when I was with you." Tears welled in the corners of her eyes. "I'm so sorry it took me so long to see that. I'm so sorry that I never opened up to you before and told you how I was really feeling, but I'm doing it now. Callan Walsh, I want to spend the rest of my life with you. I love you. Will you marry me?"

His eyes widened, but he couldn't stop the smile from spreading across his lips. "Is this real life right now?"

"Well, the ache in my knee says yes, so an answer anytime would be great," she kidded, holding the ring back up to him.

"Stand up." He reached for her and pulled her up in front of him. He wrapped his arms around her waist until she was flush against him. "Jos, all I ever wanted was to hear those words from you. Of course I'll marry you."

She grinned, throwing her arms around his neck and kissing him. God, he kissed her back like a man who'd been starving. It took everything in him to hold back and not completely devour her right then and there. Kissing her again after all this time? It was everything he'd ever wanted, and for the life of him, he couldn't remember why they'd ever stopped.

After a moment or two, he remembered where he was and pulled away slightly. "Wait . . . can I ask?"

"What?" She didn't seem to understand what he was referring to.

"Are you . . . are you pregnant?" He pointed to the room around him. "We're in a nursery."

She laughed, the same joyous sound he'd missed so much. "No, silly. This room is for your daughter. I wanted you to see that she will have a place in my life too . . . if you want that. I love you, Callan. And your future daughter is going to be a part of your life forever. I'm okay with that. In fact, I can't wait to meet her."

Callan felt like his heart was going to slide right out of his chest and hit the floor. "I would love nothing more than to have you be a part of my daughter's life."

"Then it's settled . . . you're moving in here."

This time it was his turn to laugh. "Oh, am I?"

She nodded. "It's perfect. Halfway distance between the studio where I'll be filming my new cooking show and your training center. The airport isn't far for when you're traveling. The neighborhood is in an amazing school district for your daughter . . . and any other future children you may have."

"With you," he clarified. "No one else."

"Duh," she teased. "If you knocked up someone else now, I'd chop off your balls."

He put a hand over his package. "Shit, woman."

Josie laughed and then showed him around the room, pointing out each thing that they needed to care for an infant. She'd clearly done her homework and was ready to go. Hell, this nursery here was more set up than Michelle's was at her house.

Callan sat in the rocking chair and pulled Josie down onto his lap. "Thank you, Jos. This gesture . . . it's beautiful."

"I love you, Callan Walsh," she replied, kissing him gently. "All of you."

"And I love you, Josie Gray." He kissed her back. "I'm going to marry the shit out of you."

She laughed and curled up into his lap. "Forever."

"Forever."

EPILOGUE

"Oh, my God!" Josie looked down at the puddle on the floor between her feet. "Babe!"

Her husband walked into the room a moment later. "What's up?"

Josie stared at Callan as she pointed down at the ground. "I think my water just broke."

His eyes went wide, and he started moving at warp speed. "Okay, let's get you in some dry clothes. The go-bag is ready. I'll get it in the car. Here. Here's some clothes. Put them on, and I'll be right back."

She took the shirt and sweatpants from him and worked as quickly as she could to take off her old clothes and put on the new ones. Until a contraction hit her. She groaned loudly as she gripped the edge of the bathroom countertop.

"Josie?" A little voice reached her, and as soon as she could see straight again, she looked at the entrance to the bathroom to see Alice standing there. "What's wrong?"

Callan was quickly behind her and scooped the little girl up into his arms. "Alice, guess what, baby girl?"

"What?" she responded, wrapping her arms around Callan's neck for support.

"Your baby brother is on his way here," Callan told the little girl.

She started bouncing in his arms. "He is? Where is he? I want to see him!"

"Well, he's in Josie's tummy right now." Callan pointed at her. "We're going to go to the hospital and get him out."

Josie wasn't looking forward to that at all. As thrilled as she was to be pregnant with their first child so soon after their wedding, the thought of actually pushing this giant kid out of her was freaking terrifying.

Callan reached a hand out to Josie. "You ready?"

She nodded, taking his help and waddling as quickly as she could manage toward the car. He helped her into the front seat carefully and then buckled Alice into her car seat in the back.

"Your mother is on her way," Callan told her. "Your brothers, too, but they're going to be here in a few hours because they're coming from Vegas."

Josie's mother had moved to Burbank to be closer to her when she'd found out she was pregnant. Originally, Josie had been dreading the forced closeness, but it had actually been a huge blessing. She and her mother had become quite close, really bonding, as her mother had helped her prepare for becoming a mother herself.

"I called Mommy, and she's going to pick you up at the hospital," Callan spoke toward the back seat, talking to Alice. "You excited to see Mommy?"

"I want to stay with you," Alice whined. "I want to meet my baby brother."

Callan pulled the car onto the street and headed in the direction of the hospital. "You will, but he's—"

"Ah!" Josie groaned loudly again, almost screaming as a new contraction hit her and ripped through her entire body. She wasn't sure what sin she'd committed to deserve this pain, but all she could think about was getting to the hospital and getting hooked up to drugs as soon as possible. More power to the women who could do this without all the medication, but that wasn't about to be her.

Callan reached over and squeezed her hand. "Here. I'm here. Hold on to me," he encouraged. "Crush my hand if you need to."

She chuckled wryly as the pain subsided for a little bit. "Thanks."

By the time they arrived at the hospital, she'd had two more contractions. Thankfully, the doctors and nurses worked fast. They got her hooked up to medication, and the pain recessed as a pleasant numbness took over instead.

"I'm here!" A shrill voice rang through the air as Michelle Rae waltzed into their hospital room. "How's my baby?"

"Mommy!" Alice lifted her arms in the direction of her mother.

Michelle picked her up and swung her onto one hip, kissing her temple. "Hi, baby girl. I missed you." She then turned to face Josie, who was lying in the hospital bed chewing on ice chips while Callan stood beside her and rubbed her head. "And how is your baby?"

"Doctors say everything looks great so far," Callan said. "It shouldn't be much longer now."

"That's so exciting," Michelle replied. "Congratulations again, Josie."

"Thanks, Michelle." Josie smiled at the woman whom she'd actually grown quite close to. They weren't ever going to be best friends or anything, but there was a mutual respect between them. They both loved Alice and wanted the best for her. That was all that mattered. They could certainly treat each other kindly on top of that.

"Do you want me to get you anything? I can stick around," Michelle offered.

Josie shook her head. All she needed in that moment was Callan, and he was there. "I'm good."

"If you wouldn't mind bringing Alice back tomorrow?" Callan asked. "We should be recovering by then, and I'd love for her to meet her little brother."

Michelle nodded, smiling. "Of course. I can't wait to meet him as well. Good luck!"

She then walked out with Alice on one hip and her crossbody purse on the other.

Finally alone for the first time in a while, Josie turned to Callan. "Thank you."

"For what?"

"For being the best husband and father I could have ever asked for," she replied, reaching up and caressing his cheek. "I am so blessed to have you in my life. I love you, Callan."

Callan kissed her on the forehead and leaned in closer to her. "Motherhood is making you mushy."

She shrugged. "Maybe, but it's true."

"I love you too," he replied. "I can't wait for the rest of our lives together."

Josie smiled, staring up at the man she'd married and was about to have a son with. She couldn't believe her luck or the blessings her life had in store for her. And to think . . . it had all started with burying a sex doll in the desert.

MORE MISADVENTURES

Misadventures of a City Girl
Misadventures of a Backup Bride
Misadventures of the First Daughter
Misadventures of a Virgin
Misadventures on the Night Shift
Misadventures of a Good Wife
Misadventures of a Valedictorian
Misadventures of a College Girl
Misadventures with my Roommate
Misadventures with a Rookie
Misadventures with The Boss
Misadventures with a Rock Star
Misadventures with a Speed Demon
Misadventures with a Manny
Misadventures with a Professor
Misadventures on the Rebound
Misadventures with a Country Boy
Misadventures of a Curvy Girl
Misadventures with a Book Boyfriend
Misadventures in a Threesome
Misadventures with My Ex
Misadventures in Blue
Misadventures at City Hall
Misadventures with a Twin
Misadventures with a Time Traveler
Misadventures in the Cage
Misadventures of a Biker
Misadventures with a Sexpert

**VISIT MISADVENTURES.COM
FOR MORE INFORMATION!**

ABOUT SARAH ROBINSON

Top 10 Barnes & Noble and Amazon bestseller Sarah Robinson is a native of the Washington, DC, area and holds both bachelor's and master's degrees in criminal psychology. She works as a counselor by day and romance novelist by night. She owns a small zoo of furry pets and is actively involved in volunteering in her community.